The Fantastic Freshman

The Fantastic Freshman

a novel by
BILL BRITTAIN

HARPER & ROW, PUBLISHERS

Cambridge, Philadelphia, San Francisco, St. Louis, London, Singapore, Sydney

New York

Library of Congress Cataloging-in-Publication Data
Brittain, Bill.
  The fantastic freshman : a novel / by Bill Brittain. — 1st ed.
    p.   cm.
  Summary: Miraculous luck from a magic charm grants fourteen-
year-old Stanley his deepest desire, to be a VIP in his high school,
but the exhausting and comical complications make his life miser-
able.
  ISBN 0-06-020718-3 : $
  ISBN 0-06-020719-1 (lib. bdg.) : $
  [1. High schools—Fiction. 2. Schools—Fiction. 3. Magic—
Fiction. 4. Humorous stories.] I. Title.
PZ7.B78067Fan   1988   87-35051
[Fic]—dc19   CIP
                                             AC

For all those among the faculty,
staff and students who were so friendly and
supportive during 26 years at the
ol' LJHS

Contents

Chapter 1

Labor Day Blues

Oh sure, I know what you're going to tell me as soon as you've heard my story. You're going to say that it was all my imagination, and that none of those crazy things at the beginning of my freshman year of high school really happened. Right?

Well, you'd be wrong. It all *did* happen, because of the one thing I wanted more than anything else in the world. My big aim in life was to be a Very Important Person.

It didn't matter what kind of a VIP. Any kind at all, just as long as I could be somebody special, and not just a nameless little leaf on that huge tree called the human race.

President of the United States, maybe? Nah. Sometimes people get mad at the president when they think he's done something wrong. I wanted everybody to like me.

1

A movie star? Yeah. Like one of the actors of the nineteen thirties, or the forties or fifties, when all the actors were heroes and everybody looked up to them. Being driven around in a long, black limousine and going to fancy parties and being asked for my autograph all the time were things I really thought I could get used to.

Up in my bedroom I've got five shelves packed full of VCR tapes of all the great movies of that era. Everything from Burt Lancaster in *The Crimson Pirate* to Errol Flynn in *Robin Hood*. Humphrey Bogart . . . Jimmy Stewart . . . John Wayne . . . I've seen 'em all—dozens of times.

And every time I'd watch one, I'd imagine myself being the hero.

Then I'd go to the mirror and I'd see a short kid with freckles and hair that wouldn't stay combed and ears that were too big for the rest of his head. And I'd have to be honest. I'm not the movie-star type.

How'd it be if I just rescued a baby from a burning building, or something like that? Headlines! MAYOR PRESENTS KEY TO CITY TO HEROIC STUDENT. Wouldn't that be terrific?

But as for becoming a VIP, I had a couple of things working against me. The first one was my name.

Stanley. Stanley Muffet. Now I ask you, what kind of a name is that for a Very Important Person? President Muffet? The Russians would die laughing. *Shootout in Dodge City*, starring Stanley Muffet? No way. MUFFET SAVES INFANT FROM FLAMING APARTMENT? Ridiculous.

I'd even asked Mom a couple of times if I could have my name legally changed. I gave her a choice of Dan Blake or Rick Hastings. She just laughed. Stanley Muffet I remained.

My second handicap came up the summer after I'd graduated from eighth grade.

I spent the first couple of weeks in July just being smug about the fact that never again would I ever have to return to ol' P.S. 3. Elementary school was a thing of the past. Then, all of a sudden, it dawned on me—come fall, I'd be entering the Joseph P. Alewood High School. And I'd be a *freshman*!

All the rest of that summer I went around like a convict who'd been sentenced to death. I'd get up every morning and the sun would be shining and the birds singing, and all I could think was . . . *One day closer to high school.*

And now, here it was, the first Monday in September—Labor Day. I was out in the yard, lying flat on my back under an oak tree. Up in the branches

3

a couple of squirrels were chasing each another. "Lucky squirrels," I murmured. "You don't have to go to high school."

"What's so bad about going to high school, Stanley? I'm kind of looking forward to it."

No, that wasn't a squirrel talking. That was Buster Dishy, who was leaning against the trunk of the oak tree and kicking dirt and pebbles into my upturned palm. Buster's my sometimes best friend, even if he has got a really strange outlook on life. You see, Buster never worries about anything. Whatever happens to him, he just looks on it as "a new and interesting experience." I'll bet if somebody pushed Buster over Niagara Falls, he'd be so fascinated by what was going on that he'd forget all about being scared until he got his brains bashed out on the rocks below.

"Cheer up, Stanley," said another voice, so calm and comforting that it almost made me sick. "I'm sure you'll get along just fine."

Norma Nagle was scrunched down next to the shoe of my outstretched left leg, tying and untying the laces. I say Norma's just my friend and she says she's my girlfriend, and I think you'll agree there's a lot of difference between those two words. Oh, there are times when Norma's handy to have around, no question about it. Like when you've got homework due the next day and she's the only one in the whole class who understood the assignment. Or when you've got a softball game coming up and you need somebody really good to play second base. But there are other times—like just then, underneath the oak tree—when she just refuses to take my becoming a VIP very seriously, and that drives me crazy. And once in a while—but it's been happening more often lately—she goes all soft and sweet and girlish. When that happens, I get all flustered. I think Norma enjoys getting me flustered.

But that Monday I was in a real panic, and I wasn't about to let either Buster or Norma talk me out of it. "Last year we were eighth graders!" I whined. "The kingpins of good ol' P.S. 3. We got all the special privileges, and we could keep the little kids in line and enforce all the school rules—plus making up a few just to scare 'em—and generally make everybody in the lower classes feel like they were dirt. I loved it! But beginning tomorrow . . ."

"The same things that we did to those pupils are going to happen to us," said Norma. "And it'll probably be good for you, Stanley. You always acted so high and mighty in school, it's time you got a taste of your own medicine."

"But it'll be worse, being a freshman. I heard that last year the seniors locked one freshman in his locker and it was an hour before anybody turned him loose. And during the first week they pick fights with any new student who's caught even smiling. And you've got to move around to a different room for each class, and if you're late even *once*, you have to stay after school for a month!"

"If I were you, I wouldn't believe all that stuff," said Buster. "The seniors make it up just so we'll be scared the minute we walk in the door."

"Well, it's sure working as far as I'm concerned," I told him. "I'm terrified. And Alewood High School is so big . . ."

"Over thirteen hundred students expected this year, according to the newspaper," said Buster. It was the kind of thing he could be expected to say while I was dying inside.

"I'll get lost!" I moaned. "Nobody'll know who I am. By tomorrow at this time I'll be just another name on a list someplace."

"That's your real problem, isn't it, Stanley?" asked Norma with a kind of a sneer. "This year you won't be able to be a big shot anymore, the way you thought you were at P.S. 3."

"That's right," I agreed. "That's it exactly. Stanley Muffet was not put on this earth just to be one of the common herd. I need to be a . . . a *somebody*!"

"All the 'somebody' places at Alewood High are already taken by the seniors," said Buster. "You're just going to have to wait three years until you're in the top class."

"But I can't wait. I want it now!"

With that, Norma stood up, stared down at me and shook her head sadly. Then she turned to Buster. "He gets this way sometimes, the poor thing," she said to Buster. "But he'll get over it. I understand the seniors at Alewood High have lots of ways to keep the freshmen humble."

"Yeah, let's leave him alone with his woes," said Buster. "Come on over to my house, Norma. Mom's having bridge club, and the kitchen is filled with goodies. If we're real quiet sneaking in the back door . . ."

That's when my two "friends" took off, leaving me stretched out there on the back lawn, feeling worse than Preston Foster did when they took him to the electric chair in *The Last Mile*. Even the squirrels up in the tree didn't give a hoot about my problems. One of 'em dropped an acorn that hit me right between the eyes.

As if I didn't have enough troubles, later that day my aunt Bertha dropped by our house to pay a call.

To me, a visit from Aunt Bertha is like drowning in a big barrel of honey. She loves me—boy, does she love me! Every time she comes, first I get a big slobbery kiss and a hug that would crush a moose. Then I have to sit on a hard chair in the living room while she and Mom have tea and she tells about everything that's been going on in her rooming house.

I don't know why she runs a rooming house anyway. According to Mom and Dad, when Aunt Bertha's husband died he left her more money than there is in the U.S. mint. She's been around the world a couple of times, and she owns a car big enough to hold dances in. Her house is the size of a small palace, but if she wants to rent some of the rooms out, that's her business.

Anyway, Aunt Bertha went on for an hour or so about how "her" Miss Denning has been staying out too late at night and how "her" Mr. Peckinpaw promised to paint the bathrooms for a month's credit on the rent but hasn't gotten around to it—and so on through the whole list of her "guests." Finally she reached down into her purse—a leather sack big enough to hold a bushel of potatoes—and pulled out my present.

Every time Aunt Bertha comes calling, she brings me a gift. Two months ago it was a teddy bear, and the time before that a plastic cup with I WANT MY MILK in big red letters on the side. I guess I'll always be a little baby to Aunt Bertha. Mom tells me it's the thought, and not the present itself, that counts. Maybe that's true, but I can't help wishing that sometime Aunt Bertha would bring me a model airplane or a horn for my bike.

This time, though, the present she handed me looked like it might have possibilities. It was a lump of bluish glass, shaped like a pyramid and about five inches high. Inside the glass was a tiny gold statue of a little fat man wearing nothing but what looked like a bath towel wrapped around his middle. When I looked more closely at the statue, I saw it had not only horns on its head, but four arms instead of two.

"Hey, this is neat!" I said to Aunt Bertha, who was smiling fit to bust. "I'll bet this came from some Far East religious cult with high priests and secret passwords and . . . and everything. When I show this to Buster and Norma, I'll tell 'em . . . tell 'em . . ."

Then I stopped and shook my head. I wasn't going to tell Buster and Norma anything. There was some printing below the statue that said:

BATOR-RAJ INSURANCE COMPANY
We will take good care of you

My blue glass religious symbol from the Mysterious East was nothing more than a paperweight. A sales gimmick.

"Mr. Peterson, one of my guests, moved out rather hurriedly a few days ago, owing two weeks in rent," said Aunt Bertha with a little sniff. "The glass pyramid was the only thing he left behind. I thought you'd enjoy having it, Stanley."

Terrific, I thought, gazing at the little gold fat man with the horns on his head and the four arms. If somebody else takes off, leaving a couple of pencil stubs or a bundle of dirty laundry, I'll probably end up getting them, too. I was about to tell Aunt Bertha that when I saw Mom looking daggers at me, so for once I kept my mouth shut.

Somehow I managed to sit through the rest of Aunt Bertha's visit. I even let her give me another of her slobbery kisses when she left. At supper that evening Dad gave me a long talk on how proud he was that I was going into high school—as if I had any choice—and how both he and Mom hoped I'd really try to do my best. I'm sure you've all heard the same kind of thing at one time or another. Then I felt Mom's hand pressing against my forehead.

"You're awfully quiet, Stanley. Aren't you feeling well?"

"Sure, Mom, sure. I'm just fine. Maybe a little tired." How was I going to tell her or Dad that I was scared out of my socks about going into the freshman class? What a lecture *that* would have led to.

After supper I went up to my room to watch TV and maybe do some more worrying. I put the glass pyramid on my dresser, right beside Dexter Dragon.

Dexter Dragon? Oh, he's just a big stuffed toy of green felt that I got for my birthday when I was a little kid. He's nearly six feet long, with one big black button eye (I tore the other one off the winter I had the measles). The real neat thing about Dexter is that you can push your hand down inside his mouth, and way down where his stomach would be there's a little baby dragon that you can pull out and play with.

Until I got to fourth grade, I never used to go to bed without Dexter. It was kind of comforting, lying under the blankets with that big tail wrapped around my legs and with my right arm stuck down his throat. Even now, when I'm sick or feeling bad about something, I like to have a cuddle with Dexter. Of course, you're not to let that get around. A VIP isn't supposed to sleep with a stuffed toy.

Since it was Labor Day, about all the programs on TV were reruns, so I went to my tape shelf, got *Arsenic and Old Lace* and put it in my VCR. The way I was feeling, a good comedy—especially one about dead people—was just what I needed.

Afterward I went to bed. But I couldn't get to sleep. Finally I got up, took Dexter Dragon off the dresser and pulled him under the covers with me. That did it. In five minutes I was fast asleep.

The dream I had could have won an Academy Award!

No, it wasn't about Dexter Dragon, or even *Arsenic and Old Lace*. It was about the little gold man inside the pyramid. In my dream, though, the man wasn't little anymore. He'd grown to full size, and he and I were standing in darkness, like we were in outer space or something. I suppose I should have been scared, what with those long horns and the four arms. But I wasn't.

Suddenly something came at me from out of the

darkness. It was a skull, with flames leaping out of the eye sockets and jaws that clicked together like they were ready to chew me up. But the gold man waved one of his arms, and the skull rocketed off into the darkness with a moaning sound. Next a man all in red appeared, with a pitchfork aimed at me. The gold man drove it away with a shake of his horned head. Then a monster, half eagle and half lion, and after that a great snake, with fangs the size of baseball bats. One after another creatures came, each more horrible than the last. But the gold man handled them as if they were so many pussycats.

In my dream I was so scared, I couldn't move a muscle. But as each phantom was driven off, that last line at the bottom of the paperweight kept going through my mind: *We will take good care of you.*

Then I heard a bell ringing somewhere far off. The sound kept getting louder, but I wasn't afraid anymore. I was sure that whatever happened, the golden man would make things be all right.

I glanced over at him. He was shrinking. He got smaller even as I watched. At the same time, the bell clanged in my ears loud enough to set my head spinning.

Now I was really in trouble. At my feet, the gold man, now only a couple of inches tall, was imprisoned inside the glass pyramid. *Louder* the bell rang, always LOUDER. It was . . . it was . . .

It was my alarm clock. Waking up with a start, I slammed my hand down on the button. The ringing stopped. Remembering my dream, I turned over in bed and looked at the top of the dresser. There was the gold man inside the pyramid, just as I'd left him.

Then it hit me. Today I'd be facing a new and terrible situation that not even the little man could protect me from.

I'd be going to the high school.

I'd be a brand-new freshman.

I'd be a *nobody*!

I wanted to die!

Chapter 2

Not Your
Average Freshman

My first day as a freshman at Joseph P. Alewood
High School was . . . Never in my whole life have
I had a day like . . . It was as if I had . . .

Let me tell you about it. Then you'll understand
what I mean.

I got up scared, ate my breakfast terrified, picked
up my brand-new notebook and a handful of pens
and pencils in a panic; and by the time I got to the
corner and met Norma and Buster to wait for the
school bus, I was trembling so hard I almost shook
myself out of my shoes.

All the way to school, the bus driver gave us little
lectures over his shoulder about how we were supposed to behave. Once we got there, the freshmen
were herded onto the front lawn like a flock of sheep,
with the sophomores, juniors and especially the sen-

iors looking at us like we were wads of used chewing gum stuck to their shoes.

Then the whole freshman class was led into the auditorium for more lectures. Mr. Kipp, the principal, told us he expected great things of us, and the head of each of the departments told us his or her subject was the most important one we would ever have, and then one of the coaches kind of hinted that anybody who didn't at least try out for a team sport was a cowardly cream puff, and finally a guidance counselor who had a look on his face mean enough to etch glass said he wanted to be our friend.

Then we got paraded to our homerooms. Mine was for last names M-N-O-P, and except for a few kids I'd been in eighth grade with, everybody was a stranger. But I did have Norma Nagle sitting right behind me in the second row. As soon as we sat down—in strict alphabetical order—she began whispering to me.

"Isn't this *fun*, Stanley?"

Fun? I was a nobody! Just a name on a list.

Ms. Axton, the homeroom teacher, had just started her own lecture about being on time and what to do if you were absent. Suddenly a bell clanged. I guess this was the signal for the upper classes to move around, because all of a sudden faces began appearing at the window in the door of the room. They all had nasty grins, like Bela Lugosi in *Dracula*, and one or two of 'em even dragged their fingers across their throats in a slitting motion.

Well, if the older kids were trying to scare me, all I can say is, they were succeeding beyond their wildest hopes.

After her lecture, Ms. Axton gave us each a blue sheet with a locker number and combination, and a pink sheet with a list of the periods, rooms and classes we'd be taking.

"May I have your attention!" The voice coming from the loudspeaker sounded exactly like Claude Rains's in *The Invisible Man*.

"Freshman students will now move to your first period classes. You will ignore the bells. Listen for the announcements of class changes. You will move quickly and quietly."

Ms. Axton went to the door, opened it and threw us to the wolves. Fortunately the wolves were all in class when we freshmen hit the halls. I looked at my pink schedule list.

Per. 1—Room 322—Science—Mr. Bovinski

After getting lost twice, I finally arrived at the

science room five minutes late. Mr. Bovinski, who was kind of fat, with a bald head and a little wispy beard, steered me to a seat without missing a word of still another lecture.

"Now that you know the rules of this class," he said, "let's consider our first problem in general science—the conservation of energy."

I didn't have any idea what he was talking about. All we ever did in elementary school science was collect leaves and birds' nests. With a little groan, I put my head down on the desk and closed my eyes.

All of a sudden, the little gold man I'd seen in my dreams floated in the darkness. He was holding out all four of his hands to me.

"Who can give me an example of the law of conservation of energy?" Mr. Bovinski's voice seemed a long way off.

"You there, in the first row. Can you give me an answer?"

"No, Mr. Binky."

The gold man's arms moved up and down before my closed eyes like the waves of the sea. Up . . . down . . .

"Conservation of energy. It's very simple. How about you?" he said to another kid.

No answer. The gold man held things in each of

his four hands—things that wafted through the air. Up . . . down . . .

"Or you." Mr. Bovinski's voice got louder. "Surely at least one person in this room can—"

Then I recognized what the gold man was playing with.

"Yo-yos!" I shouted.

"You! What's your name?" My eyes snapped open. Mr. Bovinski was pointing a finger at me like a loaded gun.

"Sta-Sta-Stanley. Stanley Muffet." I was going to die, for sure. "But Mr. Bovinski, all I said was—"

"You said 'yo-yos.' A perfect example of energy conservation. The energy invested in flinging the yo-yo *down* helps to bring it back *up*." He scribbled something into a book on his desk. "An A plus for today, Muffet. Keep up the good work."

The loud groans and cries of "Teacher's pet!" from the rest of the class were drowned out by the loudspeaker announcing the end of the first period.

Per. 2—Room 210—Mathematics—Ms. Darker

I got to the room with plenty of time to spare and took a decent seat, way in the back. Ms. Darker, who didn't look old enough to drive a car, let alone teach school, had a l-o-n-g equation scribbled on the blackboard.

$$B = [4\,(14-23) + 71\,(13 \times 48) - (492-4)] \times 0(3 - 1728)$$

Below it were scribbled the words *Solve for B*.

We all started messing around with pencils and paper, trying to look like we were working hard. The truth was none of us could any more solve the thing than we could fly. But we had to look busy, didn't we?

I scribbled a bunch of Z's—ZZZZZZZZZZ— like somebody snoring. Then I sat back to admire my work. "The mark of Zorro!" I whispered, figuring I was safe enough way in the back.

But that Ms. Darker must have had ears like a jackrabbit's. "Repeat that, please," she commanded, skewering me with her icicle gaze.

"Zorro!" I said in confusion. "I mean zero . . . uh . . . nothing."

"Zero—or nothing!" she cried out triumphantly. "Look at that last factor, class. Zero times anything is zero. Well done—uh—what's your name?" She leaned over her class book.

Another A+ for yours truly, Stanley Muffet.

Per. 3—Room 261—Social Studies—Mrs. Cobb

Mrs. Cobb had to be at least seventy years old, skinny and frail. But the no-nonsense look on her face seemed to say that anybody who tried something with her had better be backed up by at least six combat-ready Marines.

She began with a few really easy questions about American history. But I kept my hand down and let the others answer. I'd done enough showing off for one day. Finally she let fly with a question that stumped just about everyone.

"Name three heroes of the Battle of the Alamo."

Nobody could do it. Nobody except me.

At home, I'd watched *The Alamo*, with John Wayne, Richard Widmark and Laurence Harvey at least a dozen times. Cool as a dish of orange sherbet, I raised my hand.

"Davy Crockett, Jim Bowie and William Travis!" I piped up.

Mrs. Cobb peered at me over the tops of her glasses. "You will refrain from shouting answers before being called upon," she told me in a voice like fingernails scraping on a blackboard.

21

"Yes, ma'am."

"But your reply is entirely correct. Your name, please?"

And what do you think Mrs. Cobb put down in *her* mark book?

Per. 4—Cafeteria—Lunch

This is the period when I thought my luck had run out and I was really in trouble. Let me tell you.

At the cafeteria I got in a line about a mile long, but finally I got my food. It was okay, if you don't mind frankfurters that taste like lumber and library-paste baked beans.

When I'd finished, I decided to find my locker and see if I could open it and stash some of the armful of opening-day announcements I'd been hauling around all morning.

I located my locker, but working the combination was something else again. I tried it three times, but the metal door just sat there locked, laughing at me. Down the hall a couple of other freshmen were having troubles of their own with their lockers.

I got so mad at that closed door I finally gave it a good swift kick, and that's when I felt the tap on my shoulder and heard that sneering, holier-than-thou voice.

"Hey, frosh."

"Who?" I turned around. There stood a tall, skinny, red-haired boy, maybe three years older than me, wearing a dirty shirt, a necktie that must have been a grease rag once and an expression on his face like he'd just swallowed a rotten prune. Next to him was another boy, about the size and shape of a piano crate, with a face a mule would have been ashamed of.

"Are you talking to me?" I asked.

"You got it, frosh," said dirty shirt. "I'm Jerry Frye—*Mister* Frye to you—and this is Stonewall Lugg. We're the senior welcoming committee. And we don't like the lowly freshmen kicking the locker doors. You might hurt 'em. Right, Stonewall?"

"Yeah," said Stonewall. As soon as I heard him, I knew he had an I.Q. of about 6. But those arms of his could crush me like a grape.

"Tell the door you're sorry, frosh," Jerry Frye ordered with a smirk. "Otherwise you get this whole can of soda poured all over you."

He pulled a can of Pepsi from behind his back and jiggled it around like it was a pistol or a knife. A couple of spoonfuls slopped out and dribbled onto the hallway floor.

By this time a dozen or so big guys had gathered behind Frye and Lugg to see what was going on. I

23

looked up and down the hallway. Not a teacher in sight.

I wasn't about to go through the rest of the day wringing Pepsi-Cola out of my sweater and socks. So I turned to the door.

"I'm sorry, door," I said, feeling like an idiot.

"Now give the door a kiss," Jerry ordered.

"Yeah. Make friends," added Stonewall.

They were nuttier than a fruitcake. But what was I supposed to do?

I kissed the door.

"Very good, frosh. Now I won't have to pour this soda over your head."

"Well thanks, very . . ."

"I'm gonna pour it in your pocket, instead." Jerry reached out, yanked my pants pocket open with one hand and started tipping the can, which was in the other. That dirty tie he had on swung back and forth like wash on a line.

"Hey, wait a minute!" I howled. "You can't—"

I tried to dodge to one side. That's when my heel came down on the spot of spilled soda. My foot skidded, and I lost my balance. I reached desperately for something—anything—that would keep me from falling flat on my back on the hard tile.

I grabbed hold of Jerry Frye's necktie and held

on for dear life. The knot slid, and the loop of tie around his neck pulled tighter and tighter. Jerry dropped the can of Pepsi and yanked at the collar of his shirt. His face turned red . . . then blue . . . then purple.

Finally the tie slid through my fingers, and I dropped onto my rear end. I covered my head with my arms, just waiting for Stonewall Lugg to land on me and start caving in my ribs with those big fists of his. I hoped I'd die fast.

Nothing happened. Finally I chanced a peek up at Stonewall.

He was pointing at Jerry Frye and laughing his head off. All the other guys standing around were laughing too. Jerry's eyes were bulging out, and he was trying to shout. But with that tie pulled tight around his neck, he could hardly breathe, much less talk.

Finally a teacher showed up—an old one, wearing glasses and a sport coat that should have been a horse blanket. He took in what was going on, choked back a laugh of his own and tried to loosen Jerry's tie. But it was stuck tight.

The teacher took a knife from his pocket and cut the tie loose.

For a moment Jerry just stood there, gasping for

breath. Then he seemed to hear the laughter for the first time.

"Hey, cut it out," he gasped. "There's nothing funny. This frosh could have killed me."

"A small loss that the world could easily afford," said the teacher. "Up to your old tricks of hazing the new students, Mr. Frye?"

While everybody's attention was on Jerry Frye, it seemed like a good time for me to make my escape. I started tiptoeing off down the hall.

"Jerry Frye, licked by a little ol' freshman," hooted someone. "This oughta make page one when the school paper comes out."

"Hey, you! Frosh!" Jerry bellowed at me. "Come back here!"

Even Dexter Dragon, who's got stuffing where his brains should be, would know better than to obey *that* order. I broke into a run.

"You just wait, frosh." By now, Jerry was screaming. "Sooner or later, I'm gonna find you when there's not a teacher standing around. Then I'm gonna turn you inside out and tie you in knots. Nobody makes me look like a fool."

"Somebody already did," I heard a girl giggle from the end of the hall. "You've bullied a lot of people in this school, Jerry Frye. When this story gets around, that frosh is going to be a hero."

Me, a hero? Hey, I'd been in school only half a day, and already things were looking up.

But I couldn't help wondering what would happen the next time Jerry Frye and I came face to face. What good is it being a hero if you're dead?

Per. 5—Gymnasium—Physical Education— Mr. Elkins

The less said about gym class, the better. I'm not the physical type. But that first day, Coach Elkins just passed around a bunch of lists. I didn't know what they were for, but I signed every one I could get my hands on. Hey, how was I going to get to be a VIP if I didn't have my name plastered all over the school?

Per. 6—Room 302—English—Mr. Smee

Short, fat Mr. Smee began the class by reading us a quote from Shakespeare's *Hamlet*—"To be or not to be. . . ." Then he told us to write a paragraph of seventy-five words or less about what it meant.

I hadn't any idea. Maybe Hamlet didn't know what word to use in a sentence he was writing. Maybe he'd forgotten the number of his hotel room. Or maybe . . .

I just couldn't make up my mind. And that's exactly what I told Mr. Smee in my paragraph.

When he read some of the paragraphs to the class, Mr. Smee went absolutely *ape* over mine. "You've summed up Hamlet's problem in a nutshell, Mr. Muffet," he gloated. "The Melancholy Dane simply couldn't make up his mind. And Muffet, your use of the first person—writing as if you were the hero of the story—is a stroke of genius."

I was leading a charmed life. And I was loving it!

Per. 7—Room 119—Art—Mr. Pinkerton

With everything that'd happened before, do you really need to know about art class? Do you really want me to tell you how Mr. Pinkerton—tall and with an English accent that made all the girls swoon—picked out my paper full of crayon scrawls and how he told the class art wasn't photography and my work reminded him of the great impressionist painters like Van Gogh and Manet?

Of course you don't. Enough is enough.

Per. 8—Rm. 325—Study Hall

Three seniors came up to me especially to say hello. They told me I was real brave because of what I'd done to Jerry Frye, which is what they'd always wanted to do but were scared to because Jerry always hung around with Stonewall Lugg.

One senior girl thought I was cute.

All the way home on the school bus that afternoon I kept gloating about my first day at Joseph P. Alewood High School. I was at the top of all my classes. I'd licked the school bully. Three seniors—maybe a lot more—knew who I was. At this rate, I'd be a VIP in no time.

And to think that only a few short hours ago, I'd been afraid of the new school. But the way things were happening was a miracle.

For just a few seconds I wondered if maybe it was something other than my keen mind and charming personality that had been responsible for it all. Could it be that somewhere in the mysterious reaches of the universe there was a power that was watching over me and . . . ?

No . . . it couldn't be.

That was the first day. Sheer panic didn't set in until the second.

Chapter 3

Me? A Quarterback?

"Me? On the football team? You've got to be out of your mind. I have too much respect for my body to want every bone in it broken. A guy can get hurt playing football. He can be killed! No! No! A thousand times . . . NO!"

"Now son, you did put your name down on the list I passed around in gym class yesterday. Course, you also signed up for the locker clean-out squad and girls' field hockey, but I need football players."

"I'll clean lockers. I'll even play field hockey with the girls. Just don't make me go out on that football field. Please!"

"Why, if I didn't know you were joking, Stanley, I'd swear you were really scared. But anybody who can stand up to Jerry Frye the way you did yesterday has got the nerve I expect my players to have. Now, you just come down to the locker room after school, and I'll see you get issued a uniform. By the way, from now on, you can just call me Coach."

The voice of calm assurance in the above conversation belonged to Mr. Elkins, my gym teacher, who was also the coach of both the varsity and freshman football teams. The one doing all the screaming, protesting and quaking with fear, as you may have guessed, was me.

The first hint I got of being in hot—boiling . . . scalding—water came just as I sat down in science class the second day of school. All of a sudden that same marshmallow voice we'd heard the day before came over the loudspeaker. "The following freshman boys will report to Coach Elkins in the boys' locker room. You will move there quickly and quietly." Then the voice read off a list of names. Mine was right there in the middle.

What did I know? Maybe Mr. Elkins was going to do me a favor and excuse me from gym class. Listen, the way my luck had been running, it could have happened.

But no. When we got to the locker room, Mr. Elkins said something about "football team." Then he gave us all a bunch of forms to be filled out by doctors, parents and, for all I knew, next of kin in case of sudden death. All the other guys—who looked like they spent their spare time wrestling grizzly bears—took their forms and returned to class. I stayed. I had something I wanted to ask of Mr. Elkins, calmly and reasonably.

"Please don't make me play football!" I wailed.

"Yesterday you had grit to spare," said Coach Elkins. "What makes you so all-fired timid today?"

"We're not talking 'timid' here," I almost sobbed. "It's all-out fear. I want to live to become an adult. A nonphysical adult."

"I won't force you to play, Stanley. It's your decision. I do need all the players I can get, but I won't have it said I twisted anybody's arm. If you want to spend your next four years having everybody jeer at you and call you a craven coward and a chicken-hearted sissy, and turn their backs on you every time you walk by, plus consider you nothing but a yellow dog, you just go right ahead and quit on me."

"But I don't want . . ." Then I stopped in mid scream. I was determined to be a VIP. I decided to do it, even if it killed me.

That's how I came to be given a quick physical by the school doctor on Wednesday afternoon and then shoved out onto the football field, wearing cleats that were a mile too big and enough pads and straps inside my uniform that it felt like there was some-body else in there with me.

At the far end of the field the varsity team was practicing. I looked down there just long enough to see Stonewall Lugg brush away three players with a single swipe of his arm, like they were so many mosquitoes. That allowed Jerry Frye to plunge through the line, grab the man with the ball and throw him to the ground with a thump you could have heard in Moscow. Even though the day was cool, I began sweating, and I knew it wasn't because I was wearing so much uniform.

Mr. Clinton, the assistant coach, walked by, car-rying a clipboard. "Muffet," he snapped. "You'll play quarterback."

"I'll play all the way back if you like, Mr. Clinton. Over there behind the goalposts. I could . . ."

"Don't get funny, Muffet. Just go in there and run a play. A simple off-tackle slant."

What could I do? I trotted out onto the field, trying to look mean and tough, and knowing about as much about the game of football as I did about Egyptian hieroglyphics.

Two lines of boys faced each another. One line had on blue jerseys, but since mine was white, I got on the other side. I guess that was all right. At least nobody said anything.

I stood at one end of the white-team line, next to a boy who was crouched down as if he were looking for a dime he'd dropped. He glanced up at me and scowled. "Over there, stupid," he said. "Behind the guy with the ball."

I looked down the line. Sure enough, one player was holding the football on the ground as if he were trying to strangle it. I got behind him and wondered what to do next.

Coach Clinton blew his whistle, and I found out in a hurry.

The player with the ball shoved it at me, between his legs. At the same there was a lot of grunting and groaning as everybody on both lines started pushing at one another. All the members of the blue team were growling and showing their teeth and looking straight at me.

Finally I got it. The blues wanted to get at me, and the whites were trying to stop 'em. Come on, whites! Hold that line!

Two blue players came running around the end of the line, headed right at me. I did the most sensible thing I could think of. I threw the football to a white player standing all by himself off to my left. Let *him* get killed!

Everybody was looking at me, so when the other player got the ball, he gave me a single surprised look and started off down the field. Nobody was near him, and he would have run right into the varsity practice all alone if Coach Elkins hadn't blown his whistle.

"Muffet, come over here!" he barked.

At last! I was going to be taken off the team due to total ignorance. I tried trotting to the sideline, but in that heavy uniform it was really more of a slow shuffle.

When I reached Coach Elkins, he put his arm around my shoulder. We started walking down the field. "Nice lateral, Stanley," he purred. "I haven't seen a play like that since the Seventy-nine Super Bowl. You've got real game sense, boy."

Nice lateral? Had I done something right? It couldn't be. But then the coach went on.

"You're good, kid. Real good. Maybe it'd be a waste, playing you with the freshmen. Let's see how you do with the big boys."

"Huh?" I realized we had come to the varsity practice field.

35

But already Mr. Elkins was talking to a player built along the general lines of a tour bus. "I'm putting Muffet here in at QB. Handoff, left half, sweep right. On four. Got that?"

The coach might have been calling a square dance for all I could understand. Swing your partner round and round. Ya-hoo!

As I shuffled onto the field, I saw the players on both sides gather into a single large group. They seemed to be listening to something Jerry Frye—he and Stonewall were both blues—was telling them.

By this time I knew enough to walk over and stand behind the player crouching over the ball. Both teams were very still as the seconds ticked by. A couple of boys looked at me as if they expected me to do something.

"Count, you dummy," I heard somebody whisper.

So I counted. "One . . . two . . . three . . . four—ooof!"

The football hit me in the stomach and almost knocked me over. I clutched it to me and at the same time stood horrified as the whole white line lay down flat on the ground. A wall of big, smiling blue players came lunging toward me with nothing to stop them.

"Hey, you guys! You're supposed to protect me from . . ." Then, in a split second, I understood.

I'd been set up by Jerry Frye. No protection. I was going to—

WHAM! Stonewall Lugg, thundering up like an express train, slammed his head into my chest. At the same time, Jerry Frye wrapped his arms around my ankles, put his shoulder to my knees and pushed. The ball popped out of my hands, and I was carried backward about a mile. Finally Jerry and Stonewall threw me to the ground. I may have bounced once before every other blue player jumped on top of me. It was a gigantic human haystack, with me on the bottom.

From somewhere far off I heard the coach's whistle blow. I looked up through a sea of helmets, cleats and blue jerseys. Far above me daylight started to appear. Finally I could see Coach Elkins, peeling bodies off me like a dry cleaner sorting through a pile of overcoats.

The coach reached in, grabbed the front of my jersey and hauled me to my feet. I immediately fell back down again. All of a sudden everything about me hurt, from my hair to my toenails.

Above me a cloud did a loop-the-loop to the right, another to the left and then stood still. It occurred to me that I might live—if I didn't play any more football.

"Up and at 'em, Stan old man!" roared Coach Elkins. "You take five and pull yourself together. I want to talk with the rest of these goons."

Take five? Five years, maybe?

"Awright, awright," the coach rumbled. "What, gentlemen, is the first duty of offense on any play?"

There was an ashamed muttering from the white team. "Protect the quarterback," mumbled a couple of players.

"I can't hear you!" yelled the coach in a singsong voice.

"Protect the quarterback!" howled the team.

"But you lay down on the job, and Mr. Muffet got smeared. That pains me even more than it did him." Coach Elkins's words dripped sarcasm. "And that little trick is gonna cost you fifty sit-ups each. Come on, all you whites. Get to it!"

With a lot of grumbling and a few sneers at me, lying there on the ground, all the guys in white jerseys got down on their backs and started the sit-ups. The coach signaled to Jerry and Stonewall with a beckoning finger.

"Mr. Frye and Mr. Lugg, do you have any idea in your pointy little heads what a triumph it would be for me to have a freshman quarterback on the varsity team? So I will not have you two setting

Muffet up for cheap shots. I intend to have him out there playing this year, not lying in a hospital. So if there is any more of this nonsense—if Muffet gets so much as a hangnail, or a pimple on his nose—I will hold you two personally responsible. In that case, you may try out for the chess team or the jacks squad. But you will never—*never*—play football for me again. Is that clear?"

Jerry and Stonewall both nodded.

"Then take ten laps, just to get your minds straight. I've got to go and put Stanley back together again."

As the two players began trotting around the field in their heavy uniforms, Coach Elkins walked over and pulled me to my feet. "Are you okay, Stanley?" he asked.

Two or three months in intensive care and I'd be as good as new, I thought. But I nodded. At least for the rest of the football season, Jerry Frye and Stonewall Lugg probably wouldn't be trying to tear me limb from limb.

The coach showed me a simple pass play. When scrimmage started again, we tried it.

I leaned over the center, took the ball from between his legs and ran backward a few steps. I was real good at that running away stuff. This time my team—the whites—formed a kind of circle around

39

me to keep the blues away. Real good, whites! Do your stuff!

Way down near the goalposts I spotted a white player running across the field, with two blues chasing him. I squinted my eyes and threw the ball, expecting it to go about five feet.

It spiraled through the air like a brown bullet. It was too far ahead of the player. No it wasn't. He and the ball came together perfectly. He caught it and crossed the goal line.

My white team, the blue team and even Coach Elkins himself stood there looking at me with their jaws flapping open. "Just dumb luck," growled Jerry Frye.

"Maybe," said the coach. "Can you throw another one like that, Stanley?"

No way, I thought. I'd never even been able to hit the side of my house with a snowball. But before I could say anything, somebody tossed me another football. I kind of shoved it in the direction of the player behind the goal line.

The ball traveled forty yards on a straight line. No wobble at all. It hit the surprised player right in the chest, popped into the air and dropped to the ground.

It was weird! Wonderful, but weird!

"You're my quarterback, Stanley!" cried Coach

Elkins, giving me a slap on the back that nearly knocked me down again. "That's enough for today. I don't want you getting hurt—again. Oh, this'll be a great year for ol' Joseph P. Alewood High School!"

On the way back inside, with all the other players looking at me like I came from Mars or something, another really strange thing happened. A man even shorter than I was, wearing a bright-green suit and a hat of some kind of woven grass, came out of the stands, looked straight at me and said:

"Excuse me, young sir. Would you be one Stanley Muffet?"

He had a kind of singsong way of talking, and his hair was black and his skin olive, as if he was from the tropics somewhere. He placed both hands together, almost like praying, and bowed low at the waist.

"Yeah, I'm Stan Muffet," I said. "But who are you?"

"I am so fortunate to have located you, most athletic one. For you see, I—"

Just then Coach Elkins shoved the little man to one side. "No newspaper interviews just yet," said the coach. "Stanley's tired."

"But most plump sir, I have no wish to interview—"

"Whatever you want, it'll have to wait. Come on, Stanley."

In the showers it didn't take me long to learn the words to "The Bear Went Over the Mountain" and "Dirty Lil" and all the other songs the football players sang just to hear their own voices echoing off the tile walls. When I opened my locker to get dressed, I saw that somebody had tied my clothes in knots. I suspected it was Jerry Frye and Stonewall Lugg, who were off in a corner sneaking looks at me and mumbling to one another.

The knots were hard to untie, and by the time I got dressed in my wrinkled shirt and pants, everybody else had left. I was the last one out of the lockerroom.

The last bus had left school an hour ago. I went out through the front door, wondering how long it'd take me to walk home.

Then I heard a voice behind me. A girl's voice.

"Stanley. Stanley Muffet."

I turned around. She was leaning aginst one of the big pillars, kind of tossing her head to show off long, shiny brown hair. Her gray sweater and skirt were real tight, and I couldn't help wondering if Norma Nagle would ever look like that when she grew up.

"Are you talking to me?" I asked the girl.

"Uh-huh." As she looked me up and down, her eyelashes fanned the air like peacock plumes. "You play football very well for somebody who's so short." She wrinkled her nose like she'd smelled onions on my breath. "And so skinny."

"What's it to you how I look?" I asked, a little annoyed.

"It's very important to me. You see, you're my date for the big football dance next week."

"I'm not going to any dumb dance," I told her.

"Yes you are, Stanley Muffet. And you're going with me."

"With you? I don't even know you."

"What difference does that make?" She took a deep breath and groaned loudly. "You're nothing but a lowly freshman, so I guess I'll have to explain how things work around here. Oh, the things we seniors have to put up with."

"You don't have to put up with me. I just want to go home."

"But Stanley, according to tradition, the quarter-back of the team *always* escorts the head cheerleader to the football dance. It's been that way for years and years. And I'm the head cheerleader."

I was getting more than a little nervous. "Look, I don't want to date you. I don't want to date *anybody*."

She took my arm and began leading me toward the parking lot. "But you must!" she said in the same voice my mother uses when she starts getting mad. "If you don't, I'll look like a fool to the whole school. I won't have that."

By this time we'd reached her car—a red convertible with a racing stripe down each side. She opened the passenger door.

"Hey!" I cried out. "I don't want to—"

She gave my shoulder a hard shove and I flopped into the seat. She slammed the door, ran around to the other side and slid behind the wheel. Then she started the car and tore out onto the street like an Indy 500 racer.

"Where are you taking me?" I yelled. I was getting really scared.

"To my house. There's so little time, and I've got to teach you what'll be expected of you when you escort me to the dance."

"Your house? But my folks will be expecting me home soon. And . . . and I don't even know your name!"

"That problem at least is easily remedied. My name's Gwendolyn Keene. But everybody calls me Peachy. Do you get it, Stanley? Peachy . . . Peachy Keene."

44

Chapter 4

Peachy

Even though I had been practically kidnapped, I had to admit riding in Peachy's car *was* fun. Who wouldn't like zooming around town in a flashy convertible, with the muffler rumbling like thunder every time we peeled out from a stop and everybody looking at us and wishing they were me?

All of a sudden we zoomed up the street where I live. "That's my house—the green one!" I shouted over the noise of the engine.

"Not very big, is it?" Peachy shook her head, and her hair streamed backward in the wind. "Do you want to drop your books off?"

Before I could answer, she stomped hard on the brake. I was jerked forward against my seat belt, and the tires screeched and smoked as they skidded along the pavement. The car slid one way, then the other, as Peachy wrestled with the wheel, a big smile on her face. I don't know how she did it, but we ended up at the curb, right in front of my house.

Norma Nagle and Buster Dishy were sitting on my front steps. I guess they'd been waiting for me. Buster jerked his head around to look at the car. He saw me in it, and his eyes about popped out of his head. He and Norma got to their feet like they were zombies and came slowly down the front walk. "Sta-Sta-Stanley!" Buster gasped. "Is that you?"

Norma stared at me. Then at Peachy. Then at me again. She had the strangest look on her face—almost as if she were going to cry. "What are you *doing* in there?" she asked finally.

"I don't really know," I answered, confused. "I think it's something about a dance. You see, Peachy's the head cheerleader, and I'm—"

"A dance?" Norma glared at Peachy like she was a pile of dirty laundry there in the driver's seat. "You're going to take *her* to a dance?"

"I'm not actually taking her," I told Norma. "It's more like she's taking me. I mean, I don't really know what's going—"

"Stop sputtering like a fool, Stanleykins," said Peachy, looking down her nose at Norma and Buster. "Say good-bye to your little playmates. We really don't have time for children just now."

Naturally, at that Norma and Buster started getting mad. I was ashamed of Peachy—and of myself. Probably I should have just gotten out of the car and told Peachy to get lost. But remember, I was still in shock at the way I'd been carried off by a senior girl after football practice. Besides, sitting there on the leather seat of that shiny convertible was kind of neat.

Anyhow, I just shrugged and kept a silly grin plastered all over my face. Peachy gunned the car, and as we rocketed down the street, I heard Norma calling after us, "Ohhhhh . . . Stannn-leeeey!" Maybe the little sob in her voice was only my imagination.

Peachy Keene lived way out at the far end of town. Her house was just your basic palace, tall and wide, with turrets and gables sticking up all over. In the front yard, which was big enough to hold a carnival, a gardener was trimming a hedge. Peachy tooted the horn as we pulled into the driveway, and the gardener bowed to her. I mean that. He actually bowed, like she was a queen or something.

She pulled into the garage next to two cars, each about a block long, with shiny sides you could see yourself in. Peachy got out of the car. I just sat there looking around, with my mouth hanging open. You could have put our whole house in that garage.

"Stanley, come on!" she said, the way she might order her dog around. "We'll go inside."

We went into a hallway where a maid in a black uniform was dusting furniture. "Your father's in the library, Miss Gwendolyn," said the maid. "Shall I tell him you're here?"

"No, I'll tell him myself, Martha," said Peachy like she was a queen talking to a peasant. "Come along, Stanley."

The hike through the house was long enough to get me a merit badge in Boy Scouts. The library was filled with leather chairs and leather-covered books, and in the center of it a man sat at a leather-topped desk. He was wearing a fancy velvet jacket and smoking a cigar and writing something on paper with gold printing at the top.

"Daddy, this is Stanley," said Peachy. I must say, she didn't sound too happy about my being there.

"How do you do, Stanley?" he said, still writing away. Then he looked up. He blinked twice and stared at me like I was an insect on the head of a pin.

"Is this some kind of a joke, Gwen, or are you baby-sitting this kid for somebody?"

"Stop that, Daddy!" said Peachy angrily. "Stanley is going to be the quarterback on the team this year."

"Team?" rumbled Mr. Keene. "What team? The toddlers' squad?"

"No, Daddy. The varsity football team."

"This . . . ," said Mr. Keene, and his big belly started shaking as he pointed a pudgy finger at me, ". . . is a quarterback?"

"Yes. And as head cheerleader I'm expected to attend the season's first dance on the arm of the football team's quarterback, no matter *who* it is. Oh, the sacrifices one must make to be popular."

Mr. Keene's belly got to shaking even faster. Finally he let out a roar of laughter that boomed in my ears. "Haw, haw, haw! And this little kid is what you got stuck with, huh?"

I was getting sick and tired of those two talking about me that way while I was standing right there. It was embarrassing. My family would never have put up with such rudeness. People shouldn't act like that, even if they are rich. But scared to death in the middle of all that luxury, I kept quiet until I got another order from Peachy. "Follow me to the den, Stanley."

The den had two fireplaces, a real bearskin rug and enough animal heads on the wall to stock a zoo. Peachy stood in the middle of the room and dragged me to her side.

"Now, we don't have much time if I have to drive you home in time for dinner. So let's get started."

"Started? Started with what?"

"Stanley, haven't you heard a word I told you? If you're to be my escort to the dance, you have to learn the social niceties. I won't have it said that I went out with some clod who didn't know how to treat a girl with proper respect."

"Peachy, I'm not really sure I want to go to this dance. Wouldn't it be more fun if we just skipped it and watched television or something?"

"Have you taken leave of your senses, Stanley Muffet? This is my senior year, and I'm head cheerleader, and everything's going to be as perfect as I can make it. Perhaps you are a bit young and inexperienced, but with the proper training I'm sure you can . . ."

"I don't *want* the proper training! I want to go home!"

"Shut up! Just . . . shut up! You'll do as I say, and that's the end of it. Now, the first thing you have to learn is how to make a grand entrance with me on your arm. Stand tall, Stanley."

I tried standing tall. Peachy looked down at me with a snort of disgust.

"Can't you possibly make yourself any taller?"

"Not without elevator shoes," I said.

"That is a possibility. I'll see if Daddy can arrange something. Now, take my arm. No, not like that. That's my elbow, not a baseball bat. You've got to act masterful and protective. Remember, I'm a weak, frail girl."

I wanted to tell Peachy she seemed about as weak and frail as a SWAT team. But I didn't dare.

"Now *sweep* me into your arms as we begin the dance."

"But I don't know how to dance, Peachy."

She slapped her hand to her forehead and glared at me. "Stanley, didn't your parents teach you anything? Very well, then. Place your right arm about my waist—so. And with your left hand you grasp my . . . no, no! You just *hold* my hand, you don't squeeze it like a sponge. So then. Off we glide, and one and two and—*ow!* You stepped on my toe, you little monster!"

Standing on tiptoe, I stared straight at Peachy's chin, and we tried it again.

Twenty minutes later we were still practicing that first dance step. The toes of both of Peachy's white shoes were a dirty gray where I'd walked all over them. She was sweating like she'd been lifting weights instead of dancing. And she was calling me names that if I'd used them at my house, I'd have had my mouth washed out with soap.

I wasn't scared anymore. I was just bored. And I kept wishing that if I really *had* to learn to dance, my teacher could be Norma Nagle and not Peachy Keene.

Finally she took me home. "Good-bye, Peachy," I said as I got out of the car. "Thanks for a really . . . uh . . . interesting afternoon. But wouldn't it be better if we just called it quits? I mean, I'm a freshman and you're a senior, and . . ."

She stuck out her chin like a bulldog. "Not on your life, Stanley Muffet. It doesn't make any difference if I loathe every minute of the dance just as much as I loathe you right now. At least I will have done my duty, and I'll be able to hold my head up among the other girls. Now get out of my car, you little wretch!"

"Why, Peachy," I said in my best Cary Grant imitation. "I didn't know you cared."

I grabbed my books before she could throw 'em at me and ran off toward the house.

Of course I was late for supper. Mom did what she always does when I'm not there on time. My pot roast and mashed potatoes and carrots sat on my plate cold and jellied while she and Dad ate pie and sipped their coffee.

"Coach Elkins called me today at work, so I knew you were going out for football," said Dad. "But practice must have ended over an hour ago. Where have you been?"

"You might have telephoned, Stanley," Mom added. "We were beginning to get worried."

"There's going to be a dance next week," I began. "And . . ."

"Wait a minute," said Dad. "Let's hear about football practice first. How'd you make out?"

"I'm going to be the quarterback—on the varsity team," I told him.

"Sure." Dad and Mom grinned at each other. "And we've been made king and queen of England. C'mon, Stanley. Get serious."

"I am serious, Dad. I'm the quarterback. Honest."

Dad looked at me strangely, like I'd suddenly turned into the Creature from the Black Lagoon. "You're not kidding, are you?"

He stared at Mom, and then both of them began shaking their heads in wonder. "Tell me I'm not dreaming," said Dad finally.

"Well, you certainly can't blame my side of the family," said Mom. "The only sport they ever played was checkers."

"The nearest any of the Muffets got to athletics was when I sold tickets to basketball games in college," said Dad. "Stanley, how did this all happen?"

So I told them about how I'd signed up by mistake, and how Coach Elkins had shamed me into trying out, and how I'd made those beautiful passes. When I got to where I was tackled by the whole varsity team, Mom looked shocked. Dad just laughed.

"My son—the varsity quarterback!" he said proudly. "Wait until I tell this to the guys down at the office. They think all us Muffets have two left feet."

"It . . . it just doesn't seem real," said Mom. "Yesterday you got A's in all your classes. And today you're made quarterback of the football team. It's almost as if you . . . you were bewitched or something."

"Ah, c'mon, Mom. Anyway, after practice this senior girl picked me up, and we went over to her house and she tried to show me how to dance and . . ."

"Picked up?" said Mom in a shocked voice. "Senior girl? My, my, we are getting a bit big for our britches, aren't we?"

"And dancing, too," said Dad. "Stanley, I don't think you're quite ready for . . ."

"The next time you see that girl, you just tell her you're much too young and inexperienced to be . . . to be— Why, I've a good mind to call her parents myself. What's her name?"

"Peachy Keene. Only her real name's Gwendolyn. She lives in a big house over on Gentry Street. But . . ."

For a moment I didn't realize how quiet Mom and Dad had gotten. It was like they'd suddenly turned to stone.

"Gwen Keene . . . on Gentry Street," said Dad slowly. "Her father's Harold Keene—the banker. His bank holds the mortgage on this house."

"Oh," said Mom softly. "And didn't you tell me . . . ?"

Dad nodded. "My boss has been trying to meet with him for weeks about a big loan. But Mr. Keene has always been too busy. Yet Stanley here walks right into the house and . . ."

Then he turned to me. "Stan, old man," he said, patting me on the shoulder, "why didn't you tell us the girl you met was Gwen Keene to begin with?"

"Arthur!" exclaimed Mom.

"Now take it easy, Joan," Dad told her. "I've met

Gwen Keene, and she's not a bad kid. A little spoiled, maybe, but pretty decent. I don't think we need to worry about Stan's seeing her now and then. And when I tell the boss that Harold Keene's daughter is interested in my son, he . . . he may just give me that raise I've been asking for."

"Well . . . perhaps it'd be all right. If you say so, Arthur."

I have to admit that right then I was feeling pretty good. I was a VIP to Dad, all right. And in time I figured Mom would think so too. Now all I had to do was go to work on the rest of the world.

"With all the excitement," said Mom, kind of flustered, "I almost forgot, Stanley. Just before you got home, you had a caller."

"Oh? Who?"

"It was a stranger—a man. He was rather short and wore a green suit and . . ."

All at once I remembered the guy who'd come up to me at the end of football practice. A little knot of worry began twisting itself in my mind.

"Maybe he's a scout for the New York Giants and wants me to sign a pro-football contract," I said, forcing myself to laugh. But I couldn't help thinking of the movie *The Mask of Fu Manchu* with Boris Karloff, where an assassin with a blowgun kept shooting poisoned darts at people. The assassin looked just like . . .

"I'm going up to my room, Mom. I've got homework."

I didn't have any really. Getting it done during study hall was easy. I just wanted to be off by myself.

Mom had cleaned my room within an inch of its life. All the games and VCR tapes and maps and books I'd arranged just so on the floor were back on the shelves, and even Dexter Dragon was stretched out neatly under the dresser. I hated it when she cleaned. Sometimes it took almost a week for me to get things back into nice, comfortable, messy shape. I hardly noticed that the pyramid with the four-armed gold man inside was nowhere to be seen.

A little later I went outside, looking for Buster and Norma. I found them under a streetlight, whispering to each other. When I walked up, they greeted me like I was a can of rancid lard.

"Well, if it isn't Superman," sneered Buster. "How nice of you to spend some of your valuable time chatting with us peasants, now that you're a big shot at school."

"How come you're walking?" said Norma. "Did that big car you were riding around in this afternoon get a flat tire?"

"Hey, what gives?" I asked. "I thought you were my friends."

"Not friends, Stanley," Norma went on. "Children. Isn't that what your girlfriend called us?"

"Girlfriend? Peachy's not my girlfriend. She's just . . ."

"Stanley's a football hero too," said Buster. "Football heroes don't have time to tell their friends—who waited an hour after school and missed the bus—that they're not coming home with us mere mortals."

Suddenly Norma stuck her face right up to mine. "Then you have the nerve to ride up in that fancy car with that . . . that overdressed female!" She wrinkled up her face like she'd swallowed vinegar and batted her eyes the way she'd seen Peachy do it. " 'Say good-bye to your little playmates, Stanley,' " she went on, in a voice exactly like Peachy's.

"It wasn't my fault Peachy made me ride with her!"

"Sure, I'll bet she just forced you into that car," snorted Buster.

"She did!" I squawked. "But I—"

"Oh, Stanley!" Norma wailed. "When I saw you with that . . . that cow wearing lipstick, I could have . . ."

"Come on, Norma," said Buster, tugging at her arm. "Let's go over to my house and steal some ice cream out of the freezer."

"Good idea," I said. "Then we can—"

"Just *us two*," added Buster. "No big shots allowed."

They walked away, leaving me standing under the streetlight.

Me! A straight-A student. Quarterback of the football team. Getting ready to go out with the most popular girl in school. Mom and Dad amazed at how successful I'd become in just two days. Well on my way to becoming a high-school VIP.

So how come I suddenly felt all empty inside, as if somebody'd let the air out of me and wrung out my stomach like a wet washcloth?

Not caring who came by and saw me, I sat down on the curb and covered my face with my hands.

Then I started bawling.

Chapter 5

Student Council

On Thursday morning—the third day of school—
Buster and Norma hadn't changed any. While we
stood waiting for the bus, they jabbered away at each
other like they were having the best time in the
world. But when I tried to get in on the conversation,
they just looked at me like I was Mr. Tooth Decay
and then moved off by themselves.

When we got to school, though, I was the one
who got all the attention. The minute I stepped off
the bus, three freshman girls crowded around me,
giggling and blushing. Two of 'em wanted my autograph. The third one asked for my phone number.
Then I got called over to stand with the other members of the football team, in a private little place
they'd reserved for themselves near the bike racks,
while the rest of the kids looked on, green with envy.

I stood there like a midget in a herd of rhinoceroses, listening to the players talk about cars and dates and what colleges some of 'em would be going to next year. Not a word about old movies or fishing or anything I knew about. To tell the truth, if I hadn't had my heart so set on being a VIP, I'd rather have been with Norma and Buster.

While we were waiting for the bell to ring to go inside, Coach Elkins walked up with an armful of loose-leaf notebooks.

"These are your playbooks, team," he said, handing one to each of us. "They've got our whole strategy for the year, so don't lose 'em, and guard 'em with your lives. Have 'em memorized by Monday. Your first game's next week, and it's a big one."

I glanced through the book. Every page had a title, like "Off Tackle" or "Option Play." Then there were a lot of little X's and O's and squiggly lines and dotted lines. I didn't have any idea what all those pictures meant. But I didn't want to look like a jerk in front of the other players, so I leafed through the pages, nodding wisely.

When we got to homeroom, Ms. Axton announced that we'd have an extra ten minutes for student council elections. She spent about half of that time telling us how important the student council was to the school. Then she passed out the ballots.

Each ballot had the top offices—president, vice president and secretary-treasurer—listed, along with the four seniors who were running for each one.

"Of course, you don't know any of these people yet," said Ms. Axton. "But you'll have to put a check next to one for each office, and I *do* hope you'll vote wisely. You may, of course, write in the name of some other student if you wish to." Then she giggled, like the idea of a write-in was ridiculous.

"Our main duty today, however," she went on, "is to elect a representative from this homeroom. Are there any nominations?"

I got nominated first thing, by a fat boy in the first row whom I didn't even know. But I wasn't a bit surprised. The way things were going for me, I pretty much expected it.

"Are there any other nominations?" asked Ms. Axton when she'd written my name on the board. "No? Then Stanley will be our—"

"I nominate me!" I turned around. Norma was on her feet, glaring back at me. "Listen, girls," Norma went on. "Are we going to let the boys run this homeroom? D'you think the boys will listen to us when *we* want something done? No way! Now, I was on our council in grade school, and Stanley wasn't. Who do you think would do the better job?"

Norma got elected! I came in second—out of two. I don't mind telling you I was sore. I didn't want to be just a straight-A student and the quarterback of the football team. I wanted it all. How could Norma *do* this to me?

As the day passed, I got madder and madder at Norma. By the time football practice began, I was really boiling. I even managed to block out Stonewall Lugg on one play, just by pretending it was Norma I was hitting. When Peachy corralled me and took me to her house and we practiced dancing, I walked all over her toes—on purpose. And I was even glad when I got home late for dinner and Mom and Dad were worried. If I was going to feel lousy, I wanted other people to feel that way too.

It wasn't until Friday, during eighth period, that I found out I had bigger things in store for me than being a mere homeroom representative.

I was sitting in study hall, doing the last of my science homework. It was a report on the inventions of Thomas Edison, and since I'd seen Spencer Tracy in *Edison the Man* about five times, I had the report almost finished.

Then a student aide came in. She told me that Mr. Kipp wanted to see me in his office.

What had I done? I wondered. I followed the aide

downstairs to the principal's outer office. The secretary looked up from her typing.

"Stanley Muffet?" she said. "Mr. Kipp is waiting for you. You can go right in." She pointed to a door with PRINCIPAL painted on it in ominous black letters.

The inner office was huge, with dark walls that had pictures of cats on them. Over near the windows Mr. Kipp sat at a desk of polished wood that could have doubled as a bowling alley.

"Sit down, Muffet," he said, pointing to a chair at one end of the desk.

"Am I in trouble, Mr. Kipp?" I asked.

"No. Not in the usual sense," he replied. "However, a situation has come up, Muffet—a situation that has never before occurred in the history of Joseph P. Alewood High School. A situation involving you."

"I . . . I don't understand, sir."

"Of all the organizations in the high school, the student council is my favorite." Mr. Kipp picked up a rubber band from his desk and began stretching it between his thumbs. "I myself was council president when I was in school. And in my many years as principal here, the council has always run smoothly and efficiently."

"If this is about the student council, you've got the wrong person. Norma Nagle is our homeroom representative . . ."

"The main reason for that smoothness and efficiency," Mr. Kipp went on as if he hadn't heard me, "is that the president has always come from the senior class—a person of experience in school affairs."

"What's that got to do with me?"

"This year, however, there is a difference." Mr. Kipp stretched the rubber band longer and longer. "The president of the council will be a freshman."

"Really?" I said, kind of interested now. "Who?"

"You, Stanley!" *Snap!* The rubber band broke and rocketed across the room.

"What?" I couldn't believe my ears.

"It seems there was a tremendous write-in vote for you. Particularly among the freshmen and sophomores. Your secret campaign seems to have been highly successful." Mr. Kipp began flexing a plastic ruler in his hands.

"What campaign?" I asked. "I didn't run for the job. I don't want it."

"Perhaps you're telling the truth," said Mr. Kipp doubtfully. "Maybe the lower classes took this as a way of gaining some power over the juniors and seniors. And since your encounter with Jerry Frye the other day, as well as your exploits on the football field, has made you something of a legend around here, you would be the logical choice for a write-in.

"In any case, you won. By twenty-six votes out of more than a thousand cast. And that's why I called you down here."

"I still don't get it, Mr. Kipp." That ruler in his hand kept bending more and more.

"Let me put it this way, Stanley. If, by intent or inexperience, you were to say or do anything that might reflect discredit on the council, I would be very, *very* disappointed. Do you understand now?"

"Yeah, I think I do. All I've got to do is foul up once, and you'll have my head on a plate. Right?"

Pop! The ruler, twisted almost double, broke in two. A piece of plastic went whirring by my ear.

"I wouldn't put it quite that way. But I think that in general we see eye to eye." He took a deep breath, adjusted his tie and stuck out his hand to me. "I'm glad we had this little chat," he said, "and I wish you good luck in your new position. By the way, there's a meeting after school today. You'll need to make plans for the dance next week, after the football game."

Football! I'd forgotten all about football. "But I

can't go to a council meeting after school," I said. "I've got practice. If I miss it, Coach Elkins will be mad and . . ."

"Then you must choose, Stanley," said Mr. Kipp. "If you opt to miss one insignificant practice to attend this most important meeting, Coach Elkins will indeed be a little annoyed. But he'll get over it. On the other hand, if you were to be absent from your very first duty as student council president, it would upset me beyond words. Now then—which will it be? Don't let me influence you. It's your choice, yours alone."

"Which room does the student council meet in, sir?" I asked.

Student council meetings were held in the reading room of the school library. My study hall was right next door, and when the bell rang at the end of eighth period, I was the first one there. As soon as I walked in the door, Miss Levinski, the librarian, put a finger to her lips—she did that a lot—and motioned for me to come to her desk.

"What are you doing here?" she whispered. "School's over."

"We have a meeting of the student council," I whispered back. I don't know why all the whispering. We were the only two people in there.

"You can't have a meeting here. You haven't gotten permission."

"But Mr. Kipp said . . ."

"I don't care what Mr. Kipp said. You haven't been granted permission for a meeting in this library."

"Look, I'm the president of the council, and I've got to have the meeting someplace. Besides, the library is empty."

"Makes no difference," she breathed with a shake of her head. "You need permission."

"How do I get permission?"

"You ask me."

"Miss Levinski, is it okay for the student council to meet here now?"

"Of course. Right through the door there. I'll send the others in when they get here."

The student representatives began trickling in, until there were about forty people in the reading room. One from each homeroom, plus the officers. The juniors and seniors sat at the tables on one side of the room, and all the freshmen and sophomores were on the other. When I got up to start the meeting, the juniors and seniors glared at me. But all the

freshmen and sophomores clapped and cheered—
with one exception. Norma Nagle didn't clap or
cheer. She glared.

"I . . . I guess we're here to plan the dance for
next week," I began, with no notion of what a president was supposed to do. "Mr. Kipp said—"

"Point of order, stupid," growled a junior boy in
thick glasses. "You're supposed to call the meeting
to order first."

"Okay," I said. "I call the meeting to order. Now,
about the dance—"

"What about the minutes of the last meeting?"
chirped a senior girl. "Doesn't that come next?"

"I . . . I guess so." I didn't know what a minute
of a meeting was.

Jayne Parsons, the secretary-treasurer, read out
of a notebook a lot of things that happened last June.
Half the time I didn't have any idea what she was
talking about. "I move the minutes be accepted,"
rumbled a deep voice when she finished.

"Sounds good to me," I answered. "So let's—"

"We've got to vote on it, stupid," said thick glasses.
"All those in favor say aye."

The motion passed. I tried to bring up the dance
again. Wrong. First there had to be a treasurer's

report. Jayne read through a long list of income and expenses and took about fifteen minutes to tell us we had $5.17 in our treasury.

"I move we accept the treasurer's report," said deep voice.

"Second the motion," said thick glasses. "All in favor? All opposed?"

Again the motion passed. And as president of the student council I was feeling about as useful as a square wheel. Somehow we staggered through old business, and at last, after nearly twenty minutes, we got to the dance.

"I guess we're going to have a dance," I began uncertainly. "Any comments?"

"Yeah," muttered a fat junior boy. "What band are we gonna get?"

"Well, last year we had Raphael Zebo and the Cigar Butts," said a girl in a green sweater. "Course you little kids weren't here then." She looked over at the freshmen like they were bugs floating in her milk. "Maybe we could get them back."

"They were lousy," said thick glasses. "I want Louie Lane and his Leaf Rakers."

"Nyaaa," called out another senior. "Louie don't know any of the good music. I vote for—"

"Hold it," deep voice cried out. "This ain't gettin'

us nowhere. Let's appoint somebody to get us a band. I move we give the job to our president, Stanley Muffet."

"Hey, wait a minute," I answered. "I don't know anything about—"

"I second the motion!"

That was Norma Nagle. She looked at me with her eyes flashing and her chin stuck out.

Vote taken and passed. Just like that, I had to find a band somewhere. I didn't even know how to start.

"What about decorations?" I heard somebody say.

"I move that the president see about the decorations."

"I second the motion." Norma again.

"We've got to have tickets, too."

"I move that the president take care of the tickets."

"I second the motion." Norma was getting real good at this seconding business.

"Refreshments?"

"I move that the president—"

"I second the motion."

"Clean-up after the dance?"

"I move that the president—"

"I second the motion."

My head was spinning. I wasn't running the meeting. The meeting was running *me*. In about five minutes I was chosen to find a band, decorate the gym, get tickets made, buy refreshments with the $5.17 in the treasury, clean the gym afterward, get teacher chaperons and see that there was a policeman in the parking lot.

"Do . . . do I have any volunteers to help me out?" I gasped, with a little sob in my voice.

"I move that the meeting be adjourned," said deep voice.

"I second the motion." Norma was beginning to sound like a stuck record.

"All in favor," piped up thick glasses.

"Aye!" The shout was loud enough to bring Miss Levinski to the door with her finger to her lips. She was almost run down by the gang of council members stampeding out the door. I collapsed into a chair, feeling like I'd been mugged. I had enough work to last me the rest of my life. How was I going to do it all in just one short week?

As I reeled out of the library, Mr. Kipp met me in the hall. "How did the meeting go, Stanley?" he asked.

"It was . . . was . . . real interesting, Mr. Kipp."

I wasn't about to tell the principal what a mess I'd made of things.

"Glad to hear that," he replied. "Sometimes, when the council isn't too fond of its president, they tend to make things a bit rough for him. All the work gets piled on his back."

"Really, sir?" As if I didn't know.

"Yes, but you wouldn't allow something like that to happen, would you, Stanley?"

"Yes, sir. I mean, no!"

"Are the committees for the dance all set?"

"All set, Mr. Kipp." *And you're talking to every member of every committee right now,* I said to myself.

"Good . . . good." He draped an arm around my shoulders. "I guess I was wrong about you, Stanley," he said. "I thought your lack of experience might make the council members unwilling to cooperate with you. But it's obvious that you've taken charge and that you'll get the job done. I'm proud of you. In less than a week you've become an important person in this school."

I was an important person! The principal himself said it!

So why did I feel like a first-class idiot for letting the student council make me do all the work?

"Have a restful weekend, Stanley," said Mr. Kipp, walking off down the hall.

I went to my locker and spun the combination. Band committee, refreshment committee, ticket committee—I had more work ahead of me than the president of General Motors could do in six months. I yanked the door open.

The football playbook Coach Elkins had given me that morning slid out and fell to the floor with a loud splat.

Great. Any time I wasn't working on homework or planning everything for the dance, I'd have to memorize football plays.

Restful weekend?

Phooey!

Chapter 6

A Scare and a Helping Hand

To make my Friday at school a complete bust, Coach Elkins nailed me just as I was leaving school.

"Muffet, you missed practice today!" He said it like I'd committed a murder or something.

"Student council meeting," I told the coach. "I couldn't help it. Mr. Kipp made it pretty clear I had to be there."

"You've gotta be ready when we play Loomis High School next Friday," he grumbled. "Otherwise they're gonna wipe up the field with you, and we'll be carrying you off in a basket. How'd you like that, huh?"

Just the thing, I thought, to make me want to go out there and play the game for good ol' Joseph P. Alewood H.S.

"Well, I'll expect you to work twice as hard at practice next week. And know those plays!" Coach Elkins jabbed a finger at the playbook I was carrying.

"Study 'em all weekend if you have to."

Sure I would—when I wasn't finishing my homework and then doing everything all by myself to get the Friday-evening dance organized. Me, a VIP? It was more like Stanley Muffet—boy slave.

And when I walked outside, there was Peachy Keene.

"Stanley, I thought you'd *never* show up," she said, pouting. "Get in the car. We have lots of work to do."

Peachy didn't know the half of it.

Dancing practice was the same as always—terrible.

Afterward, in her car, we screamed at one another all the way to my house. Then Mom had tuna casserole for supper. I hate tuna casserole.

Afterward I studied the playbook. At least, I looked at the pictures in it. Finally Dad gave me a hand.

"The X's are your team," he explained. "And the O's are your opponents. Now look here—this X is you. You hand off the ball to the fullback . . ."

"Which X is the fullback, Dad?"

Finally, though, all those X's and O's and squiggly lines began to make some sense. On almost every play, I either passed the ball or gave it to somebody else to run with. Then I got out of the way so I wouldn't get killed.

The only play where I actually had to carry the ball myself was something called a quarterback sneak. On that one I was supposed to take the ball and go crashing into the line, where about a million tacklers would be waiting for me.

I decided right then and there that next Friday, no matter what, I wouldn't be calling for any quarterback sneaks.

I went to bed early, but I was awake for a long time. I lay there, looking at Dexter Dragon under the dresser and wondering if anybody else in the world had it half as rough as I did. By the light of the streetlamp coming through the window, I could see Dexter staring back at me. He didn't offer any advice.

The next day Dad had a golf date, so I took over his little office. If I was going to get anything done on the dance, I needed a telephone.

In the phone book I looked up "Bands" and then "Orchestras." The only thing listed was a symphony orchestra, and I didn't think that was quite what the student council had in mind. I decided to skip the music problem for a while and go to work on the tickets.

I called two printers. Both of 'em told me they couldn't possibly get the work done in under ten days unless I paid extra. When I told 'em I had only $5.17 to spend, one of the printers began laughing fit to bust. The other one hung up on me.

Refreshments? I found that $5.17 would get me three bologna sandwiches—with or without mustard.

By the middle of the afternoon, I wanted to put my head down on Dad's desk and start bawling. Then, just to make my day complete, Peachy phoned me.

"Stanleykins," she cooed, "I do hope you haven't forgotten to order my corsage for the dance."

"Corsage?" I sputtered.

"Yes, you know. Flowers. The quarterback always gives the head cheerleader a corsage to wear. It's expected. Now, I think I'd prefer an orchid. Don't you think that would be nice?"

"An orchid? How . . . how much is that?"

"I have no idea. But I'm sure the florist can tell you."

The florist did. Seventeen bucks. And my allowance was already overdrawn for the next three weeks.

At the rate I was going, I wouldn't get even before Christmas. I hoped Mom and Dad wouldn't mind getting homemade gifts, like the paper tracings of my hands I used to make in kindergarten.

By supper I felt as if I'd spent the day pounding rocks and I still hadn't gotten a thing done for the dance. Supper was Swiss steak, which I usually like. But Dad had played a rotten round of golf, which ended with his missing a two-foot putt on the final hole and getting razzed by the other players. Mom had dented a fender on the way home from her women's club meeting and then burned the beans. So, with the way I was feeling, you can imagine what sparkling conversation we had at the table.

Afterward, I went up to my room and watched my tape of *The Pride of the Yankees* with Gary Cooper and Teresa Wright. At the end, when Lou Gehrig walked off the baseball field and you knew he was going to die, I cried and blubbered like a baby. Maybe if I could arrange to die in some dramatic way, I thought, Coach Elkins and Mr. Kipp and the student council would be sorry for the way they'd stuck me with all this work.

On Sunday, after church, I just sat around. All the stores were closed, so I couldn't do any calling about the dance. Normally I'd have checked in with

Buster and Norma, but the way those two had been acting lately, there didn't seem to be any point in trying to talk with 'em. I read the Sunday comics and moped around and sighed loudly and generally made such a nuisance of myself that finally Mom got fed up.

"Stanley, will you get outside and *do* something?" she snapped in exasperation.

"Do what, Mom?"

"I don't know. Go for a walk. Go see your friends. Go fishing. *Anything!*"

Fishing. Good idea. There was a big vacant lot down at the end of the block, and it had trees and a little pond in the middle with fish in it. Oh, nothing you'd want to hang on the wall—just sunfish maybe six inches long. But it was something to do.

I got my pole and dug some worms from behind the garage. Then I walked down to the lot and made my way through the trees to the pond. When I got in there, I couldn't see any houses, and it was like I was a thousand miles from civilization. I wondered if I could build a little shack there and live like a hermit for the rest of my life. Let other people be the VIPs.

As usual, the fish were very cooperative. They'd bite at worms, bits of paper, lint from my pocket—

anything. I pretended I was Gray Eagle, the wise Indian guide who had to provide food for the band of settlers he was leading into the western wilderness.

"Ugh! Take heap many fish to feed white men," I said. It was silly, but it was fun, too. Of course, I didn't keep any of the fish. They were too small.

"Maybe catch heap big fish next time. Maybe shark or whale or—"

Snap! Somewhere off in the trees, a dry twig snapped. Feeling like an idiot with all that movie-Indian talk, I stood there quietly, wondering what— or who—was walking among the trees. I heard a *crunch, crunch* of feet moving through dry leaves.

Buster? Norma? Maybe one of them wanted to make up for the way they'd been treating me all—

I saw a flash of green. It was a lot brighter than the leaves on the trees. A voice called out:

"Young sir? Young sir? I saw you come in here. Where are you?"

It was the man with the olive skin I'd seen on the football field. The same one who'd come to the house while I was out, asking for me. I could see him clearly through the trees, holding that straw hat on his head with one hand and brushing branches aside with the other.

What I couldn't figure out was why he was chasing

me all over the place—especially out here in the woods.

I ducked behind a tree and tried to do some quick thinking. Then, all at once, the only possible answer popped into my head.

Jerry Frye had sent him—that had to be it! Hadn't Jerry threatened to turn me inside out and tie me in knots, that first day of school? But he couldn't do it himself because Coach Elkins had told him to leave me alone, and if he laid a hand on me, the coach would kick him off the football team—or worse.

I was absolutely sure that right now, Jerry Frye was somewhere with about a dozen other guys, setting up an iron-clad alibi while his buddy in the green suit was out here getting ready to tear my head off.

I peeked around the tree. Okay, the guy was really tiny, and being real polite with that "young sir" talk. He reminded me of Peter Lorre in the *Mr. Moto* movies, just before Mr. Moto ripped into a gang of thugs, tossing 'em around like confetti with his jujitsu way of fighting. I had to get out of there!

I dodged from tree to tree, trying my best to do it silently. Once in a while I'd step on a twig, and the man would hear me. Then he'd stop wandering in circles and move in my direction. "Please show yourself, young sir. I beg of you."

And get myself killed? No way. I edged nearer and nearer to the street. Finally I got to the sidewalk. I ran about three steps toward my house. Then I stopped.

If I ran that way—if he thought I was going home—he'd follow me, sure as shooting. I turned around and ran back the other way. Just then he popped out of the woods, right in front of me. "Please!" he cried out. "My time is precious. If you would allow—*oooof!*"

I thumped into him and knocked him down on the soft earth. Without looking back, I legged it off toward downtown. At the next corner I turned left, ran halfway up the block and dodged between two houses. There I crouched down behind a couple of garbage cans.

Sure enough, a few seconds later, the little man in the green suit came racing by. He stopped about twenty feet from me and looked around. His eyes darted this way and that, and I thought he'd spot me for sure. But then he pushed his hat down on his head and raced off.

I took backyards until I got home. I bolted through the kitchen door, panting and wheezing.

"Stanley, what's wrong?" asked Mom, who was having herself a cup of coffee.

"Nothing . . . Mom . . . ," I said between gasps. "I . . . I went fishing. Like you said."

"Fishing? But where's your pole?"

"I left . . . left it at the pond. I'll get it . . . maybe tomorrow." *And maybe never*, I said to myself. Not if that little man was out there waiting for me.

Monday was filled with things to do. And I hated all of 'em. Oh, school itself wasn't so bad. I was the top student in all my classes, and the teachers thought I was really somethin', and I was getting used to being called teacher's pet by the other kids.

But as soon as classes were done, there was football practice. First calisthenics—push-ups, sit-ups, jumping jacks—until I was so tired I could hardly stand. Then scrimmage—pass the ball, run with the ball, get tackled, remember all those plays. And Coach Elkins always screaming in my ear about how if I made a single mistake on Friday afternoon, Loomis High School might beat us and then everybody'd hate me for the rest of my life.

After practice Peachy drove me to her house for more practice—only she was even more demanding than the coach. I had to learn to hold her arm just so and be very attentive and feed her compliments all the time for the other girls to hear. But what a pain in the neck it all was! Especially since I was so pooped out from football practice.

Naturally I was late getting home for supper. So after Coach Elkins's screaming and Peachy's nasty comments about my lack of manners, Mom and Dad got their turn to pick away at me. By the time I trudged up to my room to do my homework and try to figure out what to do about the student council dance, I felt like I was in some kind of cosmic game, with me on one side and the whole world playing against me.

Just then, Mom called upstairs. "Stanley! You have a visitor!"

I was scared. Was it the man in the green suit again? But just as I decided to hide under the bed, Buster Dishy appeared at the doorway of my room.

"Hello, Stanley," he said. So I knew he was still angry. Otherwise he'd have called me Stan, like he usually does.

"What are you doing here, Buster?"

"I guess my curiosity got the better of my temper," he answered grimly. "I've gotta know what gives with you. We've been friends all our lives, you and Norma and me. Now, all of a sudden, you won't even give us the time of day. You're always too busy with the football team or hanging around with Peachy Keene."

"Buster, I—"

But Buster wasn't finished. "Norma's the one I feel sorriest for," he went on. "She really wanted you to take her to the dance on Friday. She was even going to ask you, if you were too thickheaded to make the first move. Then she saw you in that fancy car with—"

"I wish I was going to the dance with Norma, too," I said sadly. "I'm sorry she's not going to be there."

"She'll be there, all right. Her brother doesn't start college until next week. He's going to take her."

Norma was going to her first big high school dance with her *brother*? I felt lower'n the bottom of a well, not just for me, but for Norma, too. All the other girls would be meowing like cats about how she couldn't get a date and had to . . .

I couldn't stand it anymore. I threw myself down on my bed, buried my face in the pillow and started blubbering like a baby. And I was sure any moment Buster would start laughing at me.

Only he didn't laugh. I felt the mattress sink as

he sat on the edge of it, and then his hand was patting my shoulder.

"You're not acting like the big high school hero now," he said. "I've never seen you like this except when you're way over your head in trouble. Want to tell me about it?"

"Bu-but I thought you were mad at me."

"I guess I was," said Buster. "Oh, not at the old Stanley. Just what you've turned into since we've been going to high school. Always trying to play the big shot."

"I didn't try," I replied. "It—it just happened. And now I'm stuck going to the dance with that dumb Peachy Keene, and Norma's sore and—"

"All you've got to do is tell Peachy how things are," said Buster, as if it were the simplest thing in the world. "Then you go and ask Norma—"

"But I *can't*," I moaned. I told Buster about how much my dating Peachy Keene meant to my parents. "But maybe there won't be any dance to go to," I finished up.

"How come?" Buster asked in surprise.

I explained how the student council had stuck me with all the work. "I haven't been able to find a band or refreshments or—or anything."

"Maybe I can help," said Buster. "Where's a phone?"

We went down to Dad's office. Buster picked up the phone and dialed. "Hello, Dave? Buster. I need a five-piece dance combo, Friday at our high school. About eight o'clock. Sure . . . sure, that'll be fine. See you then."

He hung up. "Now you've got a band," he told me. "My cousin over at Maxton University and four of his buddies. Only two hundred and fifty bucks."

"But the council's nearly broke. We can't pay—"

"Take it out of ticket sales. My cousin's used to waiting for his money."

"Tickets!" I gasped. "We still haven't got any. And they're supposed to go on sale three days before the dance."

"I'll run 'em off for you on my computer printer at home. It's real fast, and I can have 'em first thing Wednesday morning. Now, about the refreshments . . ."

A few more phone calls and Buster had lined up a bunch of freshmen and sophomores who'd bake cookies and mix up a few gallons of punch. "Oh, by the way," he said when he'd finished, "the refreshment crew said they'd clean up afterward, too."

In less than half an hour, Buster took a load off

my shoulders that had felt like the Rock of Gibraltar. "But how come you're doing all this for me, Buster?" I asked him. "I mean, after the way I treated you and Norma . . ."

"You look awful when you get to crying," he said. "Kind of forlorn, like my puppy when we give it a bath. I felt sorry for you, that's all. And now you tell *me* something. What did you mean by that remark before about not trying to be a big shot in school? Nobody—especially no freshman—gets A's in every subject and voted president of the student council and made quarterback of the football team and all the rest of it without working his tail off. What do you take me for, Stanley—a fool? To get where you are in just a week, you'd have to be plugging away twenty-seven hours a day."

"But I didn't!" I protested. "It just . . . happened."

"Banana skins!" snapped Buster. "I do everything for your dance except play the first waltz on my kazoo, and what thanks do I get? You tell me lies. I came over here to see if somehow we could be friends again. But if you expect me to believe—"

"It's true, Buster!"

"Stanley?" Buster put his face close to mine. "Do you *swear* that you aren't trying to make all this VIP stuff happen?"

"I . . . I swear it, Buster."

"And if you're not telling the truth, may you get bunions and fallen arches and green spots popping out all over your face?"

"May I get . . . may all that stuff happen if I said one single word that was a lie. I swear!"

Buster got to his feet, swiped an arm across his forehead and stared long and hard out the window. "Then there's more here than meets the eye, Stan," he said in a hollow voice.

At least he was back to calling me Stan again. "What do you mean?" I asked.

"It's . . . like you were bewitched or something."

"That's silly."

"No, it's not. Magic *does* happen, though most folks just put it down to coincidence. But how could it happen to you? And when?"

"I—I dunno." I couldn't believe it, but suddenly I was taking Buster seriously.

"Let me see," he continued. "You were okay last week, when we were talking under the oak tree out back. Now tell me everything you did, from when you went into the house until you went to school the next day."

So I did. Aunt Bertha's visit . . . her giving me the glass paperweight . . . watching the movie in my room . . . even taking Dexter Dragon to bed with me. I'd almost finished describing that awful dream where the little gold man held off all those monsters when Buster let out a yip.

"Hold on! That's it!"

"What's it, Buster?"

"The paperweight with the little gold man inside. I'll bet my best pair of pants that's what's doing this to you. Even the motto proves it—*We will take good care of you*. You wanted to be a VIP, and it took care of you, all right. It made you one."

"It—it's ridiculous!"

"No it's not. That four-armed man must be a kind of a . . . a god or something. The question is, can we take away its power? Or do you even want to?"

Buster looked me straight in the eye. "Tell me, Stan," he said grimly. "Do you like being the high school hotshot? Is that what you really want?"

I could feel the tears filling my eyes again. "I hate it!" I yelled out. "I don't want to be a VIP anymore. I just want to go back to being friends with you and Norma and . . . and . . . But it all sounds so crazy. Are you sure . . . ?"

"Nope," said Buster with a shrug. "But there's just one way to find out. Where's that pyramid?"

I looked around the room. Since Mom had cleaned

it, I hadn't been able to find anything. "I don't know," I said. "Maybe Mom tossed it out."

"You'd better hope not." Buster began opening my dresser drawers and peering inside. "If it's gone, you could be stuck this way forever."

Buster was so convincing that I started looking around too. We searched the room and my closet, and we even turned down the covers of my bed and lifted the mattress.

The pyramid with the little gold man inside was nowhere to be found.

Chapter 7

Football Hero

All the rest of that week I couldn't get Buster's idea out of my head. Things like that were impossible. Magic spells were things you read about in books or saw in the movies, with lots of special effects. They didn't happen in real life.

But then I thought about all the crazy things that'd happened in one short week of school. Classroom genius, football quarterback, going to a dance with the most popular girl in school, president of the student council. My being under a spell was the only way to explain it.

I've gotta tell you, I wasn't too crazy about the idea of having magic worked on me. It was like my whole life was no longer under my control and somebody else was pulling the strings, and I was nothing but a puppet.

Of course, there were some advantages. I got 100

93

on the first science test. The next highest mark in the class was a 78. My English essay came back with "Good" and "Excellent" scrawled all over it. In all my classes the questions I got asked were always exactly what I'd read up on the night before, even if I'd just glanced at the book for about five minutes. And when I didn't know an answer, I'd say the first thing that popped into my head, and it'd be right—every time.

Peachy taught me how to dance—more or less. It got so she was able to shove me around the floor without my stepping on her toes very often. And I finally figured out what she wanted in the way of "manners." All I had to do was wait on her hand and foot and tell her how divine and gorgeous she looked and say dumb things like "Peachy, that's so *witty*" every time she opened her mouth, and she was as happy as a pig in clover.

The student council had a quick meeting on Wednesday morning to talk about dance-ticket sales. When I passed out the tickets Buster'd printed up for me and told about how all the work they'd stuck me with was taken care of already, everybody was surprised. Course I didn't mention Buster. The only one who probably knew about his help was Norma.

When I'd finished and everybody clapped, she thumbed her nose.

My folks were real proud of me. Mom wrote long, bragging letters to my grandparents, and Dad told everybody at his office about how I'd been made quarterback and was dating the head cheerleader, Mr. Keene's daughter.

But there were a lot of things about being a VIP that were really rotten. In my classes none of the other kids would talk to me unless they wanted to know an answer. Before the bell rang, I'd walk up to a bunch of guys talking about a neat show on TV or how they were going to get up a game of Trivial Pursuit, and as soon as they saw me, they'd stroll away like I had bad breath or something, and I'd be left there alone.

Peachy was a big pain too. She didn't know anything about old movies or fishing or any of that good stuff. All she wanted to talk about was how much her dress cost and did I know any college men I could introduce her to. It was boring!

My parents? Okay, after all those years of "Stanley, pick up your room" and "Can't you get better marks in school?" it was kind of nice to have the praise piled on for a change. But it was always in the back of my mind that it wasn't me they were praising. It was the magic of the little gold man in the pyramid.

Where *was* that pyramid, anyway? I looked and looked, but I couldn't find it.

Football? Let me tell you, during practice all that week I was good. Or maybe I should say the magic was really working. We only had about seven plays, and Coach Elkins had worked out a bunch of signals he could give from the sidelines. Most of 'em had me passing the football. I'd take the ball from the center, fade back—see all the football lingo I'd learned?—and throw.

It always felt strange, and every time I'd expect the ball to wobble about two feet. But at the same time I'd kind of *wish* where I wanted the ball to go, and it would go there. Long passes, short passes, bombs or bullets. Right on target, just about always. Then I'd get out of the way so nobody'd try and tackle me.

Trouble was, my receivers didn't have any magic working for them. They'd get blocked, or they couldn't run fast enough. Then either the ball would hit the ground, or somebody on the defensive squad would grab it. But Coach Elkins would bawl out the receivers, not me. He said I was the greatest thing since Johnny Unitas—whoever that was.

Even Jerry Frye and Stonewall had to admit I was good.

All week we practiced. Then it was Friday—the afternoon of the big game between the Alewood Lions and the Chargers from Loomis H. S.

Everybody on the team got eighth period off to go down to the locker room and get suited up. Good thing, too, because underneath a football jersey and pants are enough pads, straps and buckles to fill a truck.

I finally got everything in place under my tight pants and the blue jersey with the big number 14 on it. I thought that might be lucky. It was how old I was.

I pulled the helmet on, nearly tearing off my ears in the process. Then I buckled the chin strap and peered out through the bars of the face mask like a guy in prison. I was as ready as I'd ever be.

The whole Lions team, with me in the middle, trotted out of the locker room and across the parking lot to the stadium. We passed six yellow buses with LOOMIS HIGH SCHOOL on 'em. At a signal from the coach we began snarling and roaring, and then we jogged into the stadium, shaking our fists in the air.

A great cheer went up from the people jammed

into the seats on the south side. The cheerleaders started jumping up and down and turning cart-wheels, and two junior boys in white sweaters and blue pants were tossing Peachy back and forth like a beach ball. She had on a white sweater too, and a short blue skirt, and she looked like she was having the time of her life.

When we got to the bench, the whole team began patting one another on the back and punching arms and holding up index fingers and screaming, "We're number one!" Everybody except me. The team kind of ignored me.

I looked across the field at the Loomis team in their maroon jerseys. All I could think of was King Kong climbing the Empire State Building or God-zilla wading out of Tokyo Bay and ripping up elec-trical towers. I mean, those guys were *monsters*. One of 'em picked up a water bucket and punched it, making a big dent. Then he shook his fist at our side of the field. I just knew he was looking right at me.

Coach Elkins signaled to us, and the whole offen-sive squad gathered around him. "Awright, you guys," he growled. "I'll call the plays from the bench, just the way we practiced it. Only you'll huddle each time so those Chargers will think Muffet's calling them. Got it?"

"If he's too dumb to learn all the plays," sneered Al Kane, the fullback, "what's he doing playing quarterback?"

"Muffet'll do just fine," said the coach. "Won't you, Stanley?"

I nodded, and my helmet tipped forward over my eyes.

I pushed it back in time to see our captain, Jerry Frye, meet with the Chargers' captain in the middle of the field for the coin toss.

We won. The Chargers would kick off, and we'd receive. The kick-return team went out on the field, and the ball was teed up. The referee blew his whistle and made a big circle with his arm. The game began!

Artie Hilficker took the kickoff on our 10-yard line, clutched the ball to his blue jersey and ran it to the 25, where four Chargers smacked into him like a fleet of trucks. The ref blew his whistle, and the kick-return team ran off the field.

All except Artie. He just lay there on the grass with his arms wrapped around the ball, his eyes closed and a vacant smile plastered on his face. A team manager went out and helped him up. Artie started walking on wobbly legs toward the Charger bench. The manager had to turn him around. When Artie came off the field, he was mumbling something about how loud the church bells were. There weren't any church bells.

"Okay, Muffet!" urged Coach Elkins. "Get out there and let me see some real action!"

I didn't want to go out on that field. I wanted to go home. The Chargers had already scrambled Artie Hilficker's brains. I was going to be next.

The coach put his hand in the center of my back and shoved. I staggered out to the center of the field, trying to get my balance. The next thing I knew, I was standing right behind Dennis Cooley, the center, and both teams were lined up for a play.

A play. I looked over at the coach. He had his left fist tight against his right shoulder. A long pass down the right side.

I started calling phony signals, just to confuse the Charger defense. "Ringo Starr . . . George Harrison . . . Paul McCartney—hup!"

The football smacked into my hands, and I faded back, expecting the players on the line to hold off the Charger tacklers, just the way we'd practiced it. I set myself and drew back my throwing arm, looking for Bobby Norton, the right end.

Suddenly I couldn't see Bobby or the team or the goalposts or anything except a huge white number

58 on a maroon jersey. It was coming right at me. Then the roof fell in.

I flew through the air, with big arms wrapped around me and my face jammed against that white 58. I hit the ground with a thump you could have heard in Cleveland, and 58 came down right on top of me. It felt like every organ inside me was being crushed into a little ball of jelly.

Al Kane picked me up, shaking his head in disgust. "Quarterback?" he hissed. "You ain't nothing but a puffball, Muffet."

The ball was placed on the 17-yard line. My first play, and I'd lost eight yards.

We went into our fake huddle. I didn't have to worry about what to say. My teammates took care of the conversation.

"You're a weenie, Stanley."

"Muffet, you stink."

"Why didn't you run, Muffet? Even a yellowbelly like you should know enough to run away from a tackler."

"C'mon, puffball. The coach is calling for a long pass right down the middle. See how many yards you can lose this time."

I lost ten. Two Charger goons picked me up, tossed

me back and forth like a Ping-Pong ball and threw me to the ground. As I got up and watched with interest as the whole stadium spun before my eyes like a gigantic top, the Loomis fans went wild. From our side of the field came just one sad cry.

"Ohhh . . . Stanley!" That was Mom.

Third down, and we were on our own 7-yard line. Coach Elkins, who looked like he wanted to cry, called another long pass. Then he signaled to the bench, and Jake Kanowski, our kicker, got up and started exercising his leg.

Another huddle, and more remarks about me. We lined up. Signals.

"Trigonometry . . . plane geometry . . . algebra . . . hup!"

I took the ball and went back as far as I could into the end zone. This time, at least five Chargers came stampeding toward me. Somehow I got the idea those guys on our line weren't really trying.

To heck with this! I wasn't going to spend the rest of the afternoon serving as a punching bag for those gargoyles on the Loomis team. I quit!

I tucked the ball under my arm and ran toward the sideline. Wrong sideline. A couple of substitutes in maroon jerseys stood there. They had big hungry grins on their faces, like they were starving and I

was a juicy hamburger. I knew they weren't supposed to touch me, but I wasn't taking any chances.
I turned around.

More maroon jerseys, and this time they belonged
to players who *could* tackle me. The ball—I had to
get rid of the ball.

Way over on the far sideline, I caught sight of
Coach Elkins. Let him have the ball. I pulled back
my arm and heaved it as hard as I was able.

Suddenly there was Al Kane, our fullback, running just inside the white stripe. He watched in
amazement as the ball sped toward him. He stuck
up his arms to keep from getting hit in the face, and
the ball fell into them. All the Loomis players were
over on my side of the field, waiting to see me get
squashed three times in a row.

Al ran seventy-two yards for a touchdown. And
the south side of the stadium went wild.

I felt arms being wrapped around me, and I thought
I was about to be tackled again. But it was the guys
from our team. They lifted me up and actually carried me off the field. "We thought you were really
in trouble those first couple of plays, Stanley," said
Dennis Cooley. "How were we supposed to know
you were just faking out the Chargers?"

Good question. I didn't know myself. While I

went to the bench and got congratulated by Coach Elkins, Jake Kanowski kicked the extra point. Seven–zip, with the Lions ahead.

It would be nice to tell you how I completed a lot of passes and put a load of points on the scoreboard the rest of the first half. It would be nice, but that's not how it happened. It was like the little gold man, having given me one moment of glory, didn't want me to have any more. Up and down the field we went. I'd throw a few passes—perfect every time—to get us reasonably close to the Charger end zone, and then none of the receivers would be able to get loose, or there'd be an interception because I threw one too long, or we'd try a few running plays and lose the ball on downs, or there'd be a fumble. Fortunately, Jerry Frye, Stonewall Lugg and the rest of the defensive squad were able to hold the Chargers to a field goal.

Score at halftime—seven–three, and we were winning.

At the beginning of the second half the Lions kicked off to the Chargers. They ran it back eighty-seven yards for a touchdown. And the extra-point try was good.

Ten–seven, the Loomis H. S. Chargers were ahead.

They kicked off, and our guys ran it back to our

38-yard line. I trotted out onto the field with the offensive squad, determined to do or die for good ol' Joseph P. Alewood H. S.

I almost died—on the very next play.

The coach called a run. As soon as I got the ball, I was to slip it to Washington Dark, our right half-back. Then I'd keep fading back, like I still had the ball and was going to throw a pass.

We huddled. No more name-calling since I'd completed that first pass. Line up. Signals.

"Spencer Tracy . . . Gary Cooper . . . Clint Eastwood . . . hup!"

I took the ball, and Wash Dark brushed by me, grabbing the handoff smooth as whipped cream. He hid the ball behind one leg and kind of strolled away from the play, while I shouted and signaled to imaginary receivers. It was a perfect fake.

A little too perfect. Two Chargers kept chasing me, thinking I still had the ball. "Hold it!" I screamed finally. "I haven't got—"

Too late. The Creature from the Black Lagoon hit me high, and the Thing hit me low. They threw me down and dived on top like little kids bouncing on a mattress. I felt a ripping, tearing sensation, and then more pain than I ever knew existed went rocketing down my right leg.

Wash Dark got thirteen yards before he was tackled. I got a ride to the bench on a stretcher.

"Nothing but a simple sprain," said the doctor. "Put ice on it."

For the rest of the third quarter I sat on the bench, holding an ice bag to the back of my knee and watching the Lions and the Chargers move up and down the field. No scoring by either team.

The fourth quarter got down to its last minute, and the Chargers still led, ten–seven.

Then, a miracle. Al Kane took the ball from Juan Lopez, the substitute quarterback, and the line made him a hole big enough to drive a tank through. Off went Al, chased by the whole Loomis team. Al's not a fast runner, and they had to catch him sooner or later. Closer and closer Al got to the goal line. Closer and closer got the Charger tacklers to Al.

They caught him on the one-yard line. First and goal, with nearly forty-five seconds to go. It was a cinch.

Three plays later, our Lions had gained exactly six inches, and there were six seconds to play. Coach Elkins called a time-out.

"Muffet! Get over here!" he ordered as the team gathered around him.

"Me? Coach, I'm hurt."

"Just a sprain. Come here."

I limped over beside Coach Elkins. "This is it, Stan," he said, putting an arm around my shoulders. "You're going in there and try a quarterback sneak."

A quarterback sneak? I remembered that one from my playbook. It was the one where the quarterback could get himself killed.

"Not me, Coach."

"You've gotta. They'll be expecting it, of course. But they think we'll try going over the top of their line. Only you're small enough to go right underneath, Muffet. Nobody'll lay a hand on you."

Why did I get the impression Coach Elkins was lying through his teeth?

Like an idiot, I agreed to do it. What could I say, with all those cheering spectators behind me?

I limped onto the field, with Al Kane holding me up on one side and Dennis Cooley on the other. We lined up, with Dennis ready to center the ball and me looking right at the seat of his pants. *One big play*, I told myself, *and I'll be a VIP for sure. Come on, little gold man. Don't let me down now.*

Signals. "Dolly Parton . . . Barbra Streisand . . . Jane Fonda . . . hup!"

I grabbed the ball from Dennis's hand and plunged blindly ahead. In front of me the whole line shoved at the Chargers, trying to get me a mere thirty inches of space.

Nothing. The Charger line held like a brick wall.

Then I saw the gap between Dennis Cooley's legs. I squirted myself through it, and my knee screamed bloody murder. A maroon-clad elbow thumped into my eye, and for a moment I saw more stars than there are in all the heavens. Somebody fired a gun, and I hoped he wasn't shooting at me. Then the lights went out.

When I came to again, I was lying on the ground with my arms still wrapped around the football. My eye throbbed with pain, and it felt about the size of a grand piano. There was a roaring in my head that slowly turned to cheers, coming from somewhere in the stadium.

But which side was cheering? Had I made it or . . . ?

I looked down at the football. Across its center was a white streak, rubbed from the goal line. A precious few inches of pigskin stuck into the end zone.

The Lions had won the game! And I was a hero. Fans poured out of the stands, and everybody from Mom and Dad to Coach Elkins to the mayor was crowding around me and patting me on the back and telling me how great I was. It was heaven!

Peachy Keene wriggled her way up beside me and put her lips to my ear. I could hardly wait to hear her tell how proud she was of me.

"Oh, Stanley!" she pouted. "With an injured knee and what looks like a monumental black eye, you'll be an abomination this evening at the dance. Oh, the embarrassment . . . the degradation! How could you *do* this to me?"

"Does . . . does this mean you don't want to go to the dance with me?" I asked. The way I was hurting, I just wanted to go home and soak in a hot bath for about two weeks.

"I will be by in my car to pick you up at seven fifty-five on the dot," she snarled between clenched teeth. "And don't you *dare* keep me waiting even a single second, Stanley Muffet!"

Chapter 8

The Dance

In the locker room after the game all the players crowded around to congratulate me. Or at least most of them did. Jerry Frye and Stonewall Lugg were conspicuously absent.

Frankly, I just wanted to be left alone. I ached all over, and my right leg hurt like crazy every time I moved it, and my eye was nearly swollen shut. After I'd showered and changed, I limped out to the parking lot, where Mom and Dad were waiting for me.

Dad shook my hand and said he was proud of me, and Mom cuddled me in her arms. "Poor Stanley," she crooned. "Does it hurt much, dear? We'd better stop at Dr. Rauch's office on the way home."

"Cut it out, Mom," I protested. "I'll be fine." All the same, that hug felt pretty good to me.

"Nothing broken," Dr. Rauch told Mom and Dad after he'd examined me. "Just some pulled muscles in that leg and a classic black eye. But Stanley's not going to want to do much walking for a few days."

"A few days?" I said. "I've got to go to a dance . . . in about two hours."

"Stanley, if Dr. Rauch says . . . ," Mom began.

"Let him go and accept the applause of his adoring public for winning the game," said the doctor. "He won't be doing much dancing, but it won't hurt for him to sit and watch the others. Here, Stanley. You'll be needing this."

He handed me a cane. Great. One look at that cane and Peachy would have a fit.

After a quick bite of supper I soaked in a hot bath for a long time. Then I got dressed in my best suit. Mom had to help me get my pants on. My leg hurt every time I moved it.

When I was all set and had my hair slicked down, I limped to the mirror in the hall for a look at myself. My eye was completely closed, and it was all black and yellow and every other color of the rainbow. And because of my leg I was kind of tilted to the right. I looked uglier than Charles Laughton as Quasimodo in *The Hunchback of Notre Dame*. I didn't really want to go to the dance with Peachy. I just wanted to stay in bed until I stopped hurting and resembled a human being again.

At exactly five minutes before eight o'clock Peachy pulled up in front of the house and honked her horn. Mom gave me the white box with the orchid in it—paid for with three and a half weeks' allowance—and kissed me on the cheek. "Be good, dear," she said.

Dad handed me the cane.

I hobbled down the steps and out to the curb. Peachy, sitting behind the wheel in a long dress of white satin, stared at me like I was something that'd crawled out from under a rock. "You look disgusting, Stanley," she snapped.

What could I say? She was right.

I was just pushing and hauling myself stiffly into the tiny front seat when I heard a voice coming from the darkness behind us. "Young sir! Wait, please. We must—"

I knew who it was—the little man in the green suit. Didn't he ever give up? I didn't know what he wanted, and I had no intention of finding out.

"Step on it!" I barked at Peachy in my best Richard Widmark voice.

After a single surprised glance at me, Peachy stepped

on it. The car roared away from the curb. Under the streetlamp behind us the little man waved his hands and called after us.

"Stop, young sir . . ." Peachy took the turn at the end of the street on two wheels, like she was driving a getaway car for the mob.

By the time we got to the dance the gym was already full. It was all decorated with big paper footballs and goalposts, and at one end Buster's cousin and his band were standing in the middle of a tangle of instruments, wires and amplifiers, playing music loud enough to drown out an erupting volcano. Couples in suits and fancy dresses were hopping around the dance floor.

I showed our tickets at the door and walked in with Peachy on my arm. To tell the truth, she was propping me up so I wouldn't stumble, but nobody had to know that. I tried spinning my cane in the air the way Fred Astaire might do it, but then my bum leg collapsed under me, and I fell down. Peachy hauled me to my feet and muttered through the smile she had plastered on her face a few words you couldn't find in the dictionary.

Suddenly the music stopped right in the middle of a number. The band played a single long chord, and the lead guitarist took a microphone out of its holder. "Ladies and gentlemen," he said, and his voice echoed through the amplifiers, "presenting the man of the hour. Just entering our victory dance is Stanley Muffet, who scored the winning touchdown this afternoon. And on his arm is the lovely head cheerleader, Gwen 'Peachy' Keene!"

The whole gym went wild. There was cheering and foot stomping and whistling and . . . and everything. As we walked out onto the dance floor, several freshman and sophomore girls teetered toward me on high-heeled shoes, smiling and batting their eyes and plucking at my sleeve.

Peachy gave a yell like Tarzan after a bad day with the elephants. "Get away, you little demons! Scram!"

The girls all moved back, glowering at Peachy. She skewered me with a hateful stare. "Wasn't that disgusting, Stanley?"

I don't know. I kind of liked it.

Jerry Frye and another senior boy began whispering to Peachy in voices so low that I couldn't hear them. Peachy smiled at them and brushed her fingers against Jerry's cheek and took the other boy's hand. "A bit later, perhaps," she murmured to them. "Oh, he won't be any trouble. I'll just . . ." She put her lips to Jerry's ear. After listening to Peachy, he looked right at me. Then he laughed out loud.

Peachy led me to a far corner of the gym, where there was a beat-up, overstuffed chair borrowed from the faculty room for the evening. "You sit here, Stanley," she said. "I'm sure you'll be very comfortable."

"But I don't want to . . . ," I began.

"You must rest your leg, since your injury has made a mockery of all those dancing lessons I gave you," she insisted. "Now sit down!" She poked me hard in the chest with her elbow.

I staggered back, my knees hit the chair and I toppled into it. "Ow!" My leg let me know that it didn't like such treatment.

The springs in that chair must have been busted, because I ended up almost sitting on the floor with my knees up around my nose. On both sides the chair arms were walls that I could barely peer over. It was like being packed in a big, padded box.

Right away, Jerry Frye walked up to Peachy. "If you've got the midget taken care of," he said, "how about a dance?"

"Of course, Jerry," cooed Peachy. "Stanley won't mind. Will you, Stanleykins?"

Before I could do anything but sputter, Jerry put

an arm around Peachy's waist. Then he reached toward me with the other hand. "I'll just take that, little boy."

He grabbed my cane.

"Hey!" I yelled. "You can't . . ."

I tried to get up. But getting out of that broken-down chair was like climbing out of a well. I lifted myself an inch or two by pulling on the arms.

"Ow!" Pain knifed down my right leg, and I sank back down, sweating and trembling. I tried again. More pain.

Finally I had to face it. Until I got help I was trapped in that chair. I leaned back, hoping I wouldn't have to go to the bathroom anytime soon.

"Hi, Stan. How does it feel, being the school hero?"

It was Buster. He was with Barbara Dennison, a girl we'd both known back in eighth grade.

"Buster tells me you're under a magic spell of some kind," said Barbara.

I looked daggers at Buster over the chair arm. "Why don't you broadcast it to the whole world? Put it on the evening news, for Pete's sake."

"Why not?" said Buster with a shrug. "It's not your fault. You can't help it if you're bewitched."

He made it sound like some kind of a disease.

"You're just guessing that it's magic," I grumbled. "But maybe it's just me. I mean . . ."

Buster shook his head. "Maybe you could make top grades in all your classes on your own. *Or* you might have the dumb luck to become quarterback on the football team. *Or* by some fluke you might be elected student council president. *Or* you might get to date the head cheerleader. But *all* of 'em? No way. It has to be magic. Otherwise the whole world is completely nuts."

"It's spooky," said Barbara. "But it must be kind of fun, too. I mean, who wouldn't like being the big hero of the whole school?"

Me? A hero? Here I was, with a black eye and a leg I could hardly stand on, trapped in a chair while the girl I'd brought to the dance was off scouting out senior boys. Some hero.

"Did you have any luck finding that pyramid with the little man?" Buster went on.

I shook my head. "And on top of everything else," I said woefully, "there's this guy . . ."

I told Buster and Barbara about the little man in the green suit who'd been chasing me around all week.

"Hmmm." Buster scratched his head. "It could

be a football scout from some college, I suppose. No, they'd wait at least until you were a junior. I don't know, Stan. This whole thing is weird. Have you thought about listening to what the man has to say? Maybe it has to do with the missing pyramid."

"Yeah, and maybe he wants to kill me or sell me into slavery or something," I sneered. "I want nothing to do with that guy."

"Stan, you've got to find that pyramid. Then we can find out if it's the thing causing all your problems."

"I've looked everywhere. It's . . . it's gone."

"If you don't locate it," said Buster in a worried voice, "you could end up being king of the world. And the unhappiest guy alive."

"Unhappy?" said Barbara. "But I thought anybody as popular as you are, Stanley, would be . . ."

Over the top of the chair arm I peered at her through my one good eye. "Is this the face of a happy man?" I moaned.

Just then, my troubles increased by one—or two. Norma Nagle walked over to my chair, escorted by her brother, Ray. Ray was about six feet tall and handsome enough to make Robert Redford jealous. And he was wearing a tuxedo.

Ray used to make little toys for us kids and tell

us ghost stories and even buy us ice-cream cones sometimes. A real swell guy.

But when I saw him standing there holding Norma's hand like he owned it, I wanted to kill him. All of a sudden *I* wanted to be the one holding Norma's hand.

"I'm sorry you hurt yourself and can't dance, Stanley," she said. It was the first time she'd spoken to me in a week. And she sounded about as sorry as if she'd won the Irish Sweepstakes.

"Put a lid on the sarcasm, Norma," said Buster. "I told you, Stan can't help what's happened to him."

"Oh, sure," replied Norma, curling her upper lip. "All that stuff about magic. What a line of drivel! I've read better stories on bubble-gum wrappers. But you boys have to stick together, don't you?"

I sat up real tall so my face stuck over the chair arm. "Norma, it might be . . ."

She peered at me in the dim light. "Stanley, your poor eye!" she cried. "It's so . . . so . . ."

She moved closer and stuck out her hand. I thought she was going to sock me. But she just brushed her fingers around my sore eye, very gently. "Oh, that's terrible! Does it hurt much?"

Yeah, it did. Especially where she was touching it. But I didn't want her to stop.

"My goodness, Stanleykins! You certainly don't lack for entertainment with all these people about you. But I'm back now."

It was Peachy. She stood there beside Jerry Frye, and she pretended to be talking to me. But she was staring at Ray Nagle like a hungry dog eyeing a pot roast.

"And who is this attractive man?" Peachy sidled up beside Ray and brushed the sleeve of his tuxedo lightly with one hand.

"Surely you remember Ray, Peachy," said Norma. "You chased after him most of last year when he was a senior here."

Peachy ignored that. "What are you doing with yourself these days, Ray?" Her eyelashes fluttered like a flag in a high wind.

"Getting ready for college," said Ray. Meanwhile, in the background, Jerry Frye looked ready to kill. And he was still carrying my cane.

"College?" Peachy might have been announcing that she'd discovered gold. "I'd love to hear all about it. Why don't we go off somewhere quiet? Just you and me."

"Lay off, Peachy," said Norma. "He's my brother and my date for the dance. You came with Stanley."

"Now, now, young lady," said Peachy as if she

were talking to a three-year-old. "You must learn to be more genteel and unselfish."

"Unselfish?" Norma snapped. "First you grabbed off Stanley, and now you're going to work on Ray. You're nothing but a two-bit man snatcher."

"Why you little brat!" Peachy snarled. "For two cents, I'd—"

"Try anything with me, and I'll punch you right in the nose!" snapped Norma. "Though you keep it stuck so high in the air, I might not be able to reach it."

I found myself wishing Norma would do just what she'd threatened. At the same time, I noticed Jerry Frye, angry and red in the face, stalking off across the dance floor.

"Now just calm down, ladies," said Ray Nagle. "No sense ruining a good dance with some petty argument. Norma, I did come with you, that's true. But just to be polite, maybe I could save a dance or two for Peachy."

"You take one step on that floor with that . . . that overdressed bag lady," said Norma, "and I'm telling Mom and Dad how you dented the fender of their car and blamed it on the parking lot man. I will, Ray. I swear it."

Ray looked at Peachy, shrugged and shook his

head. Norma had the goods on him for sure.

"Which one of you characters is giving Peachy a hard time?" rumbled a voice. Everybody turned around. There stood Stonewall Lugg, with Jerry Frye kind of hiding behind him. I figured Jerry didn't want to take on Ray Nagle by himself. So he'd brought up reinforcements.

"That's the one, Stonewall," said Jerry. "The one in the tuxedo."

"Hey, wait," said Ray. "I wasn't trying to . . ." He took a step toward Stonewall.

"Don't crowd me, man," said Stonewall. He put his hands out and pushed Ray away.

"Hey, don't push me, fella," said Ray angrily. "I don't like it."

"Oh? Too bad about that." Stonewall stuck out his hands again. Ray grabbed a wrist.

"Leggo!" Stonewall ordered. Ray held tight. Stonewall slapped at Ray's head with his free hand. Ray ducked, still holding that wrist.

"Leggo, I said!" howled Stonewall. Meanwhile, Peachy just stood there, scared of a scene but still excited that two boys were about to fight over her. Buster and Barbara crouched behind Peachy, and Norma hid behind all the others.

Ray and Stonewall moved in a little half circle,

with Ray's hand still clamped to Stonewall's wrist like grim death.

"Okay, wise guy. You asked for it!" Stonewall shot a fist out at Ray's head. Ray crouched, and the fist went over his head, close enough to part his hair. Then he let go of the wrist and brought an uppercut square into Stonewall's belly.

"Oof!" Stonewall lurched back . . . right into Peachy.

From there on, it was like a falling row of dominos. Peachy tumbled into Barbara, who toppled into Buster. Buster staggered into Norma, whose balance was already precarious on her high heels. With arms waving and shoes clattering, Norma sat down hard.

Smack on my left leg. The *good* one.

I heard a dull *thunk*. At the same time, more pain than I'd ever felt in my life screeched up and down my leg. It was as if somebody had stuck a sword in my knee.

I remember thinking that with one leg sprained and the other one broken, I'd need a wheelchair just to get around.

Then I fainted.

I woke up in an ambulance. Pain was ripping through both legs, and I was bawling like a baby. Through the circular window in the side of the ambulance I could see everybody from the dance gathered outside in the school parking lot.

A man in a white uniform looked down at me. "Take it easy, young fellow," he said. "It's a simple fracture. We'll get it set as soon as we get to the hospital."

"But Mom . . . Dad . . . ," I mumbled.

"They've been notified. They'll meet us at the emergency room. As soon as a cast is put on that leg, they can take you home. Now don't try and talk anymore. I've given you a sedative. You'll be asleep in a few minutes."

"But . . ."

"Don't look so scared. This kind of thing happens all the time."

It wasn't the broken leg that terrified me.

It was the face that suddenly appeared at the little round ambulance window—the face of an olive-skinned man who wore a hat of woven grass.

Chapter 9

"We Will Take Good Care of You"

Saturday morning. Dad was at his office, and Mom was downstairs. We'd won the football game, the dance was over—brought to a sudden end when I'd broken my leg—and except for a little homework I didn't have a responsibility in the world.

And there I was—stuck in bed, with both legs out of commission. The right one throbbed painfully, and the left one had a heavy cast on it from above my knee down to my ankle. Talk about bad luck— I had had enough to last me the rest of my life.

Oh, there were some good things. After Dr. Rauch came by to check my busted leg—he'd looked at the X rays and said I'd be as good as new in a few weeks—the whole football team, except Jerry and Stonewall, paid me a visit. Mom about had a fit, with all those big guys clomping up the stairs and crowding into my room. But they brought the ball

I'd won the game with, and they'd all signed it. That made up for some of the discomfort I was going through.

A little later the cheerleaders dropped in, all in uniform. They all wrote their names on my cast, and a couple of the girls did theirs in lipstick. I twisted my head back and forth, looking for Peachy. I guess she had other things to do. Still, I'd have loved all that attention if I hadn't needed to nearly be killed to get it.

Norma and Ray Nagle and Buster Dishy showed up around lunchtime. Ray apologized for his part in the fight and said he'd send me a beer mug from college as soon as he got there. I could see Buster didn't want to say anything about the glass pyramid while Ray was there, so he just darted looks about the room and then stared at me. I caught the question he was trying to ask—had I found the pyramid?— and I shook my head sadly.

Norma didn't seem to know whether or not she was still mad at me. But at least she was talking, and that was a step in the right direction. She plumped up my pillows and helped me sit up, and when Mom brought in a bowl of soup, Norma insisted on feeding me, like it was my arms and not my legs that were injured. She poured about half the soup in my nose and ears and onto the pillows. But it was still kind of nice, having her look after me that way.

When they left, there was just me, sprawled out helplessly on the bed, with nothing in reach except my schoolbooks and a pile of comics. I didn't want to do my homework, and I didn't want to read about the Incredible Hulk. I was feeling so low, I didn't even want to watch a movie. If this was what being a VIP was all about, I'd sooner be a nerd.

Around two o'clock Mom stuck her head into the room. "Stanley, I simply must go to the store," she said. "We're out of everything. Do you want me to get one of the neighbors in to look after you while I'm gone?"

"No, Mom," I replied with a sigh. "I'll be fine here."

"I thought I'd drop by Aunt Bertha's, too. Just to let her know what happened to you. Are you sure you'll be all right?"

"If you mean do I have to go to the john, the answer is no," I said. "I just want to be left alone. But Mom?"

"Yes, Stanley?"

"You might ask Aunt Bertha if she's got any more of those pyramids. You know—like the one she gave me, with the little gold man inside."

"I'm sure she doesn't, dear. If you recall, she said a Mr. Peterson left it when he moved out. Why, is it important?"

Important? My whole life depended on it. Only I couldn't tell that to Mom. She'd think I was nuts.

"No, it's not important."

"Be a good boy, Stanley." Mom closed the door, and I could hear her walking downstairs. A few seconds later she backed the car out of the driveway, and I was alone in the house.

It's funny, the things you can hear when you're in a house alone. On the dresser beneath which Dexter Dragon crouched, my alarm clock ticked merrily away. From the bathroom I could hear the *pock pock* of water dripping into the bathtub, and through the open window came the sounds of wind in the trees and an occasional car going by. From the kitchen, right below my room, I heard the hum of the refrigerator and a door softly opening and closing, and . . .

A door opening and closing? That couldn't be right, unless . . . unless somebody'd just sneaked into the house!

Maybe Mom had come back for something she'd forgotten. No, I'd have heard the car. A neighbor, paying a visit? But a neighbor would have shouted out to see if anyone was home. I hauled myself to a sitting position, and I could feel the sweat popping out on my forehead.

There was somebody in the house with me—somebody who shouldn't be there!

I listened without breathing. Sure enough, I could hear hushed footsteps, like whoever it was, was walking on tiptoe. Through the kitchen—into the living room—on the stairs . . .

I had to do something. I had to phone the police. But how could I get to the telephone? I couldn't even walk.

Now the footsteps had reached the top of the stairs. They were coming toward my room. My tongue was as dry as sawdust as I stared at the closed door to the hall. All I could think of was old Scrooge, waiting for Marley's ghost to appear.

Slowly the doorknob turned with a scratching sound. The door inched open. Then I heard the whispery voice: "Ah, young sir. Excuse stealthy entrance, please."

A head poked itself around the door. Above the olive-skinned face a hat of woven grass was cocked over one ear.

It was the little man who'd been chasing after me all this time. The one I figured Jerry Frye had sent. And now he'd caught me.

I was going to get clobbered for sure. I'd seen enough Fu Manchu movies to know I didn't stand a chance. Just let me die quick, I thought, yanking the blankets up to my chin.

The little man approached the foot of the bed, clasped his hands in front of him and bowed deeply. "Let me introduce myself. I am Bator-Raj."

That was the name on the glass pyramid! "You—you weren't sent here by Jerry Frye?" I asked.

"Who Jerry Frye? I not know such a person. I am Bator-Raj, and I come to reclaim my property, which you now possess."

I took a deep breath and let it out slowly. He wasn't going to pulverize me. All he wanted was—

The pyramid! But I didn't have it anymore. When he found that out, he was still liable to . . .

I had to stall. That's what victims did in all the movies. Maybe Mom would come home. Maybe another visitor would drop in. I needed to keep the man talking.

"You—you want the glass pyramid, I guess, huh? The one with the little gold man inside."

I watched the man's hands, waiting for him to dig a gun from his pocket like Peter Lorre in *The Maltese Falcon*. But he just smiled.

"Not a man inside pyramid," he said. "That a durkee."

"A turkey?"

"You not listen good, young sir. I said 'durkee.' "

"Oh. I'm sorry. But with that accent of yours, it's hard to understand . . ."

"I speak seventeen languages, young sir. How many you speak?"

"Well . . . just one. But I'm going to take beginning French next year."

"So. Back to subject. A durkee, young sir, is a creature much like leprechaun or troll. But leprechaun and troll do bad and mischievous things. Durkee do good. Bad not happen until after."

"But what's all that got to do with . . ."

The man moved to the side of the bed and sat down. So that was it, I thought. He wanted to get close enough to strangle me. I wouldn't die without a fight. I'd . . .

"Young sir, if I ask you to return pyramid, you have right to ask why. So I tell you. But if you keep interrupting, we gonna be here until next week. Can I tell story in own way, please?"

"Sure, sure. Tell me the whole thing. Take your time."

He began talking to me in a low voice.

"I come from Pol [the man began]. Pol is a small kingdom, only ten mile long, three mile wide, near where China, Burma, India, come together. Very few people ever hear of it.

"As boy I train in carving the wood. Make statues. But all the time, I have dream that one day I live in United States America. Have house with real windows and not just holes in walls. Drive big car. See tall buildings. Pay taxes. I wanted to do all these things.

"But Bator-Raj very poor. I know only way I get to United States America is if durkees help me.

"Durkees live in deep forests. But they have power to give you one thing you want more than anything else. I carve many statues of durkees. Put them all over kingdom of Pol. Even give one to king.

"Durkees see statues and decide to help poor Bator-Raj. One day I wake up in little hut and there beside me is glass pyramid. And captured in pyramid is gold durkee. I very happy. For that same day, king call me to appear before him.

" 'I send you to United States America,' king say.

'Cost lots of money, but you make statues there, sell to big stores in New York City, Washington, D.C., Akron, Ohio. Make money, repay Pol. And if people like your statues, stores order more. Soon everybody in Pol to be carving statues. We become rich country.'

"So I go United States America. But once durkees give me wish to be there, all else is unlucky, as they give one thing only.

"No stores buy my statues. Nobody even know me. Soon I sleeping on park bench, stomach rumbles alla time from no food. I gotta have money from somewhere.

"But only thing I have for sale is pyramid with durkee statue. Most people think that not worth very much.

"Then I get idea. Although pyramid have no more power to do me good, it still can help somebody else. One day I talk to man—man named Peterson, rents room, other side of this village. He steeplejack. Paint steeples, flagpoles, everything way up high. Mr. Peterson love his job more than anything. Work outside in fresh air, look down on whole world, feel like a mighty king. Only thing, he get to thinking one day maybe he fall. Then, end of fine job. Could even be end of Mr. Peterson altogether.

"I know durkee statue will protect Mr. Peterson. So I paint company name on pyramid and say I will sell him insurance. For five hundred dollar, he be sure he won't get hurt in fall.

"Mr. Peterson very suspicious, but I talk convincing. In little while he give me hundred-dollar down payment. I give him little pyramid.

"I not see rest of money for long time. Then one day Mr. Peterson fall off church steeple. Zoom! Straight down toward ground.

"Durkee take care of Mr. Peterson. But it work in way so you not really know they do magic. Parked next to church is truck, delivering cushions for seats inside. Whole rest of load on truck is big mattresses. Down come Mr. Peterson, land flat on mattresses. Nothing hurt. Not even hair mussed up.

"After that, Mr. Peterson believe I got magic to protect him. He pay me rest of money, real quick.

"Little while later, no more work for Mr. Peterson around here. He get hired by factory in Indiana to sit in gloomy cellar and rub smelly wax on furniture. Mr. Peterson hate to take such a job, but at least no danger of falling. So when he leave house of woman named Bertha, he leave pyramid behind. Bertha woman find it, give it to you, Stanley Muffet. Now you understand what happening to you?"

As the little man finished his story, he spread his hands wide. My first feeling was one of relief. He wasn't out to kill me after all. He just wanted his pyramid back.

"So that's what 'We will take good care of you' means," I said. "The durkees will give you one thing you want more than anything else. For you it was getting to the United States. For Mr. Peterson, it was not getting hurt in a fall. And me, I wanted to be a big shot in school."

"Durkee arrange it like always," said the little man, "so it look like coincidence, with no magic involved. But magic there, just the same."

"Then Buster was right!" I said in amazement.

"Who Buster?" he asked with a shake of his head. "There never been such a boy like you for talking about people I not heard of. First Jerry Frye, now Buster. All craziness."

"Speaking of craziness," I said, "if you were so anxious to get in touch with me about your magic paperweight, why didn't you call me on the telephone or send a letter or something, so I'd know you were coming. Why'd you have to come sneaking around after me and scaring me half to death?"

"Telephone? You mean plastic box with wire, you talk to it an' it talks back? Oh no! I try it once, push little buttons, get place called Moscow. Never again. And no letter as I not write the English good, even if I speak it with preciseness. So I try and see you face to face, but you keep running away."

Bator-Raj glanced down at my leg in the cast. "But you not run so much now, huh? Okay, where is pyramid?"

"I can't give it to you."

"You gotta. Pyramid is mine. Important I get it back."

"You don't understand. It . . . it's lost."

He slapped a hand to his forehead. "Oh, oh! Big trouble!"

"What do you mean, 'big trouble'?" I asked.

"Every time durkee do good thing for someone, he do bad thing as well," Bator-Raj answered. "I get to come to America—but I hate it here. Mr. Peterson not hurt in fall—but now he no longer have fine job in fresh air, way up high. You not in fine shape either, I bet."

"Your durkee did a real job on me. I'm the greatest VIP that Joseph P. Alewood High School ever saw. And my life's been a mess since the first day of school."

"If you want things back like they were before you got durkee, Stanley Muffet, I am only person who can help you."

"Help me? How?"

"In Pol, I learn mystic spell that take away all durkee power. Very special spell, hard to do. To be used only when durkee making things more than terrible. Like now, huh? But to cast spell, I first need pyramid—quick! Otherwise things get worse and worse."

How, I wondered, could they get worse than they were now?

Bator-Raj took a card from his pocket. "This motel where I stay. You find durkee, let me know, fast! Use telephone, if you must. I be brave, pick up plastic thing on wire to talk to you."

With that, Bator-Raj turned and started for the door. "Wait!" I called.

"Why wait?" he asked. "You use time to remember where you put durkee. If him all gone, you become unhappiest person on face of earth."

He slipped through the door of my room like a

shadow. I heard his feet shuffling down the stairs, and then the back door opened and closed. I was alone again. And I was doomed to become the most famous, the most powerful . . .

. . . and the most miserable student who ever attended Joseph P. Alewood High School.

Chapter 10

Just Another Freshman

For a long time after Bator-Raj left, I just lay
there, staring up at the ceiling. It just wasn't fair, I
kept thinking. Less than two weeks ago—on Labor
Day—I'd told Norma and Buster about how I wanted
to be a big shot when I got to high school. And just
because Aunt Bertha picked that exact day to give
me the glass pyramid, I was . . .

No, that wasn't quite right. I'd wanted to be a
VIP for as long as I could remember. Even in first
grade, when I was hall monitor, I got a kick out of
wearing a big paper badge and standing at the head
of the line whenever we went somewhere. No matter
when I got my hands on the durkee, it would have
been the same.

So now it had happened. And what was the result?

The other freshmen didn't want anything to do
with me because they figured I was too stuck-up. I

had to admit that they were right—I was.

The upper classes didn't want anything to do with me because I was too young.

Buster Dishy, the only other person who knew what was going on, felt sorry for me. I hate it when people feel sorry for me.

I couldn't stand thinking about how I'd treated Norma. That hurt more than anything else.

In school, I was the top student in every subject. As a result, I never got credit when I did a really good paper or had the right answer in class. It was just something people expected of me.

I was the quarterback of the football team—and I couldn't stand playing football.

I was president of the student council, and I got stuck with all the work while the representatives laughed at me and hoped I'd be a big failure.

I had taken Peachy Keene to the first big dance of the year—where she'd promptly ditched me to go off dancing with Jerry Frye and then make a play for Ray Nagle just because he was going to college.

Right there on the bed I made a big discovery. I'd never really wanted to be a VIP. What I'd wanted was the *glory* of being a VIP—all the good stuff. But the responsibility and work were just too much for me to handle. There didn't seem to be enough time anymore—time to go fishing and hang out with Buster and Norma and watch old movies and do any of the other things *I* wanted to do.

I started wondering whether everything that'd happened to me was really a dream. I mean, whoever heard of a man in a grass hat sneaking into their bedroom and telling a story about a place called Pol and durkees and a steeplejack who fell on a truckload of mattresses?

I closed my eyes . . . and in my mind I saw the gold durkee from the pyramid. It stood there in the darkness with its four hands on its two hips. It was laughing at me!

I jerked about in the bed, and both legs started hurting something fierce. Oh, I was awake, all right.

"Hi."

The voice came from out in the hall, and for a second I thought Bator-Raj had returned. But it was only Buster.

"Your mom's home," he said as he entered my room. "She let me in downstairs. I thought I should come back and cheer you up. You look like you could use it. How are you feeling?"

"Lousy," I replied mournfully.

"Maybe you should take something for the pain in your legs," said Buster. "Did the doctor give you any—"

"It's not my legs, Buster. It's . . . it's . . ."

That's when I broke down and started bawling. I didn't want to cry in front of Buster again, but I couldn't help it. Buster gave me a Kleenex and then just stood there until I got control of myself again.

Then I told him about Bator-Raj's visit. "So I guess you were right all the time, Buster," I ended up. "And now I'm stuck."

"Not if we can find that pyramid. Let's look again."

"We went through this room with a fine-tooth comb the other day. Mom must have thrown it out. It's probably down at the dump right now, buried under a few tons of garbage. We'll never find it. Besides, I can't get out of bed. How am I going to—"

"I'll look," Buster replied.

He did, too. Tossing Dexter Dragon onto the quilt beside me, he peered beneath my dresser and looked under the bed. Then he went through each dresser drawer. The closet . . . my camping trunk . . . the bookcase. Buster even peered inside the VCR.

Nothing.

"It's no use, Buster," I moaned. "I'm doomed."

With that, I reached out and scooped Dexter Dragon into my arms while Buster searched among the video tapes. I lay there, my single good eye staring into the one button eye on Dexter's cloth face. With a little sigh, I crammed my arm down Dexter's throat, just the way I used to when I was little.

My fingertips scratched the little baby dragon down there in Dexter's stomach. Closing my eye, I petted its tiny soft back and toyed with the felt spines on its back and stroked the flat, hard surface of . . .

Flat? Hard? But the baby dragon was all soft and lumpy. Then what . . . ?

I yanked my fist out of Dexter's mouth, clutching the thing I'd touched down there. Then I opened my good eye v-e-r-y slowly, excited but still scared that it wouldn't be . . .

But it was! There was the pyramid in the palm of my hand. I stared at it, scarcely able to believe my good luck. Mom must have shoved it in there just to get rid of it when she cleaned the room last week.

Funny, but I couldn't help thinking that the little durkee inside seemed to have changed position. The way I remembered, all four arms had been out-stretched. But now they were on its hips. It was bent forward slightly. And it was laughing—just the way I'd imagined it a couple of hours ago.

What did I care? I'd found it—that was the important thing.

"Buster! Here it is!"

Buster turned around and peered at the little gold man curiously. "You mean *that* little thing caused all your troubles?" he asked.

"Yep. But it's all going to be over in just a little while. Now here's what I want you to do. . . ."

I gave Buster the pyramid and the card from the motel where Bator-Raj was staying. While I was explaining how Buster had to get out there as quickly as possible, I must have said "Don't drop it!" and "Be careful not to lose it!" a hundred times.

The next hour and a half was about a million years long.

Finally I heard the front doorbell, and then Buster talking with Mom. I hoped it wasn't about the durkee—she'd never have believed in it.

Buster came up the stairs, two at a time, and burst into my room. "That was the weirdest thing I ever saw in my life," he said.

"What was?"

"Bator-Raj working over that pyramid. First he put on some kind of a bathrobe thing, with half-moons and stars and triangles all over it. Then he lighted some incense that smelled like burning tires.

Finally he began a long chant while he was waving his hands above the pyramid."

"He was removing a curse, Buster. Did you expect him to sing 'April Showers'?"

"But Stan, he did the last part of the chanting while he was standing on his head!"

"Don't be silly. How could he balance himself on his head if he was waving both hands over the pyramid?"

"He didn't use his hands to balance—just his head. Right there in the middle of the room. Straight up, like an electric pole. It's true, Stan. I swear it. Anyhow, after that, he sprinkled some kind of powder over the pyramid like he was putting salt on it. Then he polished it with a cloth that looked like a tiny carpet. A few more minutes of chanting, and that was it. He handed the pyramid back to me and started packing to go home to Pol."

"Did he say everything's going to be okay? That it's all finished?"

Buster looked at me with an odd expression on his face. "Not quite, Stan," he said.

"What do you mean, 'not quite'?" I asked. My stomach started tying itself in knots again.

"I mean Bator-Raj said that you have to do the last part."

"*What* last part?" I asked in a shaking voice. "Tell me."

"First," said Buster, yanking the pyramid from a jacket pocket and presenting it to me like it was a diamond or something, "you have to hold this in both hands and say, 'I cast away your power.'"

I cupped the pyramid like a glass baseball. "I cast away your power!" I cried.

"Good. Bator-Raj said that cancels out the durkee's magic over you. But to keep it from coming back, you have to—"

"Coming back?" I howled. "What do you mean, coming back? Is there a chance the gold man will still—?"

"Not if you do what I tell you."

"And what's that?"

"You have to drop that thing into a stream or a river or a lake or somewhere in water. Water keeps the durkee weak so it can't start bugging you again."

It sounded crazy. But I had Buster fill a little sand pail from my closet with water and bring it to me. "This is just until I can get out of this bed and find a better place to drown it," I said, dropping the pyramid in with a plop.

It would be nice to say that right about here, lightning bolts shot down from the ceiling, and sparks came up from the floor, and the whole room was filled with an unearthly yellow fog, and I sprang out of bed, completely healed. But it just didn't happen that way. I was still lying there, with one broken leg, one sprained leg and a black eye.

The only thing different was that I felt like about a million problems had been lifted from my mind. In spite of my injuries, for the first time since high school had started I was *happy*!

For the next week, I didn't go to school. School came to me. The first three days, Buster brought my assignments along with reports of what was going on at good ol' Joseph P. Alewood H.S.

"Coach Elkins figures you won't be able to play football anymore this season," he said on Monday. "So he took Jerry Frye off the defensive squad and made him the quarterback. Jerry's not doing too good. I watched practice for a while, and he got smeared, almost every play. It looks like a bad year for the team."

"That's nice," I said, with a big grin plastered across my face.

"And by the way, Peachy Keene said to tell you not to even think about taking her out again because you're too childish and immature. Right now she's got a thing for Stonewall Lugg."

"Those two deserve each other," I replied.

More good news on Tuesday. Mr. Bovinski gave me a D− on my science report. "Less than adequate" was what he'd scrawled across the top of the paper. I knew that with work I could get a C or maybe even a B for the term. But the boom days of A+'s were over.

On Wednesday Buster came in with a long face. "Guess what," he said with a sad shake of his head. "Mr. Kipp found an old rule that the school board made back in 1940. It says the student council president has to be either a junior or a senior. So I guess you're kicked out. They'll be holding new elections on Friday."

Buster began ticking things off on his fingers. "No honor roll. No football. No Peachy. And now, no student council president. No more being a VIP, Stan old man. Sorry about that. I guess from now on you're just another freshman." Then we both laughed ourselves silly.

On Thursday, Norma Nagle brought my work home to me. "Buster kept telling me how you'd been enchanted by the pyramid," she said. "I didn't believe him. But he says you've got it here—in a bucket."

I pointed to the sand pail, and Norma peered down at the gold man under the water. She reached for it, but I grabbed her hand. I kept holding it. Norma didn't seem to mind. In fact, she had a big grin on her face.

So I guessed we were back to being friends again.

"All that time I was under the spell, Norma," I said, "I didn't like myself one bit. So I don't blame you for being sore at me. I'm just glad it's over. Tell you what—how about you and me going to the movies tomorrow after school?"

"Oh Stanley, I'd love to! But you can't even get out of bed. How can you . . . ?"

I pointed to my shelves of movie tapes. "Easy. This'll be our theater. *Son of Frankenstein* and *House of Dracula*. Okay?"

"No, Stanley."

"No? You mean you're turning down my invitation?"

"Oh, I'll be glad to come. Only I'll bring tapes from *my* collection."

"You've got tapes, too? Hey, neat! What'll we be seeing?"

"Bette Davis in *Now, Voyager*, and *Intermezzo* with Leslie Howard. He's a musician, and he's in love with . . ."

"Love stories? You want me to sit through three hours of love stories?"

"They're beautiful, Stanley. And I'll bring the popcorn."

What could I say? Norma makes the best popcorn in the world.

Oh yeah, one more thing. Bator-Raj told Buster that I was to put the pyramid under water, and that would keep the durkee from doing any more harm— right?

Only I don't think that part of the spell came out the way it should have.

Oh, I'm okay, but . . . well, let me explain.

After my broken leg mended, I took the pyramid to that pond down the street where I go fishing. I threw it in.

I've been down there a lot of times since then. But I've never been able to catch one single fish, even though they used to fight one another to bite on my hook. Oh, they're in there. I can see 'em swimming around. And if you toss bread crumbs or something on the water, they'll go after it like a bunch of miniature sharks.

But they never bite on anything that has a hook in it.

We Will Take Good Care of You.

Think about it.

And think about those fish. Look at all the awful things that happened when I had the durkee.

What do you suppose is going to happen to those fish?

Poor fish.

About the Author

Bill Brittain enjoys writing books in which playfully mysterious forces are afoot. *The Wish Giver*, a 1984 Newbery Honor Book, is set in Coven Tree—a town where wishes come true. *Devil's Donkey* also takes place in Coven Tree. Both of these books were named ALA Notable Children's Books, as well as *School Library Journal* Best Books. In Mr. Brittain's first book, *All the Money in the World*, a boy captures a leprechaun who grants him three wishes. The book won the 1982–1983 Charlie May Simon Children's Book Award and was adapted for television as an ABC–TV Saturday Special. And the fast-paced mystery *Who Knew There'd Be Ghosts?* was a Children's Choice for 1986 (IRA/CBC). Mr. Brittain's most recent book, *Dr. Dredd's Wagon of Wonders*, is a companion volume to *The Wish Giver* and *Devil's Donkey*.

Mr. Brittain is also the author of over 65 mystery stories, which have appeared in *Ellery Queen's Mystery Magazine*, *Alfred Hitchcock's Mystery Magazine* and several anthologies. He and his wife, Ginny, live in Asheville, North Carolina.

CLIPPING YOUR POODLE

IN THIS BOOK, Mrs Sheldon and Miss Lockwood have put on paper a great deal of the knowledge that was imparted to the many students who attended the celebrated Poodle Management Courses which they held for some years at the Rothara Poodle Kennels. After some hundreds of students had taken this Course, the authors retired from such concentrated activities, removing to a delightful spot on the River Pang in the Thames Valley where they are now continuing their great interest in poodle breeding with a small but very select kennel of Miniature and Toy Poodles.

Mrs Sheldon and Miss Lockwood have been breeding poodles for nearly twenty years and the information which they have compiled in this new book is the result of much study and a great deal of experience. Like their previous book *Poodles*, this new handbook is primarily written for the novice-owner-breeder and should prove equally helpful and instructive.

CLIPPING
YOUR
POODLE

by

Margaret Rothery Sheldon and
Barbara Lockwood

with diagrams by
Barbara Lockwood and
Ann Brown

W. & G. FOYLE LTD
119-125 CHARING CROSS ROAD
LONDON WC2H 0EB

ISBN 0 7071 0169 7

First published 1960
Reprinted March, 1961
Reprinted September, 1961
Reprinted February, 1962
Revised Edition August, 1962
Reprinted February, 1963
Reprinted October, 1963
Reprinted June, 1964
Reprinted November, 1964
Reprinted April, 1966
Reprinted May, 1966
Reprinted July, 1967
Reprinted July, 1968
Reprinted November, 1969
Reprinted 1976

Printed and bound in Great Britain by
REDWOOD BURN LIMITED
Trowbridge & Esher

Contents

Acknowledgements

The Authors wish to extend their grateful thanks to Miss Bourne of Messrs Thomas Fall, (London), Frasie Studios, (Chicago), and Mrs Margaret Worth for photographs lent and supplied; Miss Ann Brown for drawing many diagrams; Miss Margaret Sherson for again typing the manuscript; and all individuals and firms who have been so helpful in supplying information and loaning equipment.

Foreword

IN WRITING THIS BOOK, we would like to stress that it is primarily intended for the novice owner-breeder-exhibitor, and also for owners of the companion poodle who wish to make an efficient job of clipping their own poodles.

We feel sure that with a little practice, a certain amount of patience and a careful study of the directions and diagrams we have provided, the novice will quickly become expert in this most fascinating art of poodle clipping. Those who plan to own a Poodle Beauty Parlour may find a few tips that will help them in the relative sections of the book, but those who already have established Beauty Parlours will know (or should know) as much and more than we do of the subject. Therefore, again we stress that this is a companion volume to our first book *Poodles* and intended for the novice.

All measurements given in diagrams are for Miniature Poodles and should be proportionately increased for Standard Poodles and decreased for Toy Poodles.

Also we must point out that white poodles have been used almost exclusively in the photographs and diagrams not because we have any great bias for this colour, but simply because whites are particularly photogenic, and styles and points which we wish to illustrate do show up more clearly in a white poodle than on a black or coloured one.

We hope our readers will find this handbook interesting and helpful, and we particularly hope that some of the ideas and suggestions we have put forward may save poodles from unnecessary hurt and discomfort from the hands of those people who do not know the many little ways in which the whole procedure of the poodle's toilet can be made a thing of pleasure instead of something to be dreaded.

Margaret Rothery Sheldon
Barbara Lockwood

CHAPTER ONE

Equipment for the
Private Poodle Owner

Approximate Cost—Care of Equipment

BEFORE one can start on the job of satisfactorily clipping and trimming poodles, it is essential that a small amount of money should be spent on equipping oneself with good workable tools. These need not cost very much, and the small outlay repays one a hundredfold. Certain equipment is really essential:

1. A pair of hairdressing scissors, from 12/6d to 25/-.
2. Two good steel combs, 5/- to 8/6d.
3. A grooming brush, 7/- to 9/-.
4. A pair of Electric Clippers, from £6 to £25.
5. A pair of Hand Clippers, from 22/6d to 42/6d.
6. A pair of Nail Clippers, from 7/6d to 15/-.
7. Hair Spray from 6/- to 25/-.
8. Hair Dryer from £3 to £9.

1. SCISSORS: These should be of the hairdressing type, 6½" or 7", and we have found from experience that Belgian, French or German scissors have the best tempered edge to the blades, and last longer. These can be purchased from about 12/- to 25/-. When the blades become blunt, it is a simple matter to have them re-ground and set, and this costs 2/- a pair.

2. STEEL COMBS: A 7" double comb, i.e., one that has half the comb with fine teeth and half with coarser teeth, is invaluable. The fine part is used for combing out the ears

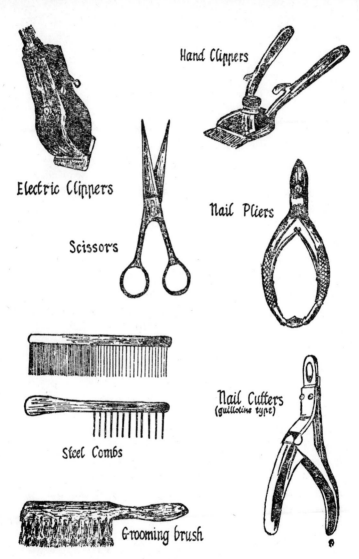

Hand Clippers

Electric Clippers

Scissors

Nail Pliers

Steel Combs

Nail Cutters
(guillotine type)

Grooming brush

Diagram 1 – Grooming and Clipping Equipment.

14

and top-knots, and any short parts, while the wider teeth are used for combing the long hair and mane. These cost about 6/-. A second comb with wide teeth and a handle is most useful for freeing a poodle's coat of matts prior to really getting down to the job of bathing and clipping. It is advisable to get good quality combs while you are about it, and those made of solid brass with tapered steel pins and chromium plated overall are most satisfactory. The cheaper nickel plated combs are not satisfactory, as the nickel peels off in time and catches the dog's hair, thus pulling out strands and generally ruining the coat.

3. GROOMING BRUSH: We have found that the 'Addis' hair brush is excellent for poodles, as it is just stiff enough to be effective and not too hard to pull out the coat. These can be obtained for about 8/-. However, when using one it is essential that the brush be held quite straight when grooming, and not turned upwards with each stroke as this latter procedure will again pull out the hair.

4. ELECTRIC CLIPPERS: There are many on the market and prices range from about £6 to £25. It is absolutely a matter of choice, but for those keeping up to three poodles, we do not think you can do better than purchase a pair of Horstman Electric Clippers. These are quiet and efficient and as there is an adjusting lever for altering the depth of cut this obviates having to change the cutter head. They are to be obtained for £8. However, a word of advice here – it is essential that these clippers should be well brushed out with an oily tooth-brush after use, and well oiled *before* and *after* use with a thin machine oil like ' Three-in-One ' oil or sewing machine oil. If they are put away after clipping without brushing and oiling, a small amount of moisture from the dog's hair remains and quickly sets up rust, and next time the clippers are required for use they will stick and catch, and

give endless trouble. They should also be kept in a warm dry place when not in use, as damp causes much trouble.

If you want a more powerful clipper we would suggest you turn to the chapter on Beauty Parlour equipment which gives you fuller details of other clippers, but of course these are comparatively much more expensive.

5. HAND CLIPPERS: If you have electric clippers it is not essential to have hand clippers as well, but there are a small minority of dogs who will not tolerate electric clippers and thus it is advisable to have a hand pair by you. These can be purchased for about 15/- to 30/-. Reliable makes are Burmans or Browns. The size for the fine clipping on a poodle is either 00 or 000.

6. NAIL CLIPPERS: There are two types – the ordinary nail pliers which are very useful, and you would be advised to get a strong pair while you are about it. Probably 5″ size, priced at about 16/6d. Alternatively, there is the Guillotine type which most poodles dislike *less* than the pliers. Nearly all poodles heartily dislike a manicure, but we have found that even the most difficult dog will tolerate the Guillotine type. These cost about 17/6d.

7. HAIR SPRAY: This is another valuable piece of equipment, and can be purchased very cheaply from Woolworths, Boots, etc., or you can easily make up your own from pieces of rubber tubing, tap junction and a small spray.

8. HAIR DRYER: This again is an essential as it is impossible to get a neat finish on a poodle's coat with rough towel drying. An ordinary Hair Dryer like the G.E.C. or Morphy Richards are perfectly suitable for a very small number of dogs, but for frequent and constant use we feel you would be wise to buy a dryer made for the job such as the Forfex as this undoubtedly has a longer life, a stronger ' blow ', and does not become

clogged with hair. A dryer stand is again a great help as you can then set up the dryer in the position you want, freeing both hands for holding and combing. This is most useful when shampooing wriggling puppies.

Most of this equipment can be obtained from Messrs. Diamond Edge Ltd., of 126 Gloucester Road, Brighton, and they will send you a most interesting illustrated price list entitled *Animal Grooming Tools*, on application. Another source of supply is from Spratts, of Bow Road, London, E.3, or Messrs. Brookwick, Ward & Co., 8 Shepherd's Bush Road, London, W.6.

If you can collect together this list of equipment, you should be all set to start clipping your poodle. This list is, of course, specifically compiled for the private poodle owner but if you want more comprehensive equipment we suggest you also study Chapter IX.

The authors would like to make it clear that the foregoing prices apply to England only. In the U.S., Canada and other countries prices may be completely different and subject to variation.

CHAPTER TWO

The Basic Clip

*Method of Using Clippers – Correct Lines for Face – Clipping the Feet
Shaping the Tail – Avoiding Clipper Rash*

THE first essential when clipping a poodle is to groom the dog thoroughly all over, so that you are able to take your comb right through the hair. If you are going to start clipping professionally, I am afraid you will find that a great many owners bring their poodles to you in a very tangled and matted state, but it is essential to get these tangles freed before you start clipping or styling a dog. Also it is absolutely *essential* that the poodle shall be free of tangles before he is bathed, as if not, the hair will go into a thick carpet as soon as the dog is wet, and this is well nigh impossible to free afterwards, and even coarse electric clippers will jib at shearing this off. In these days of high powered electric clippers it is possible to shear off a slightly matted dog with the coarse cutter head, but certainly if you have only one or two poodles, and if you carry out your own clipping, then your poodles should never get into a matted state, and need the drastic treatment of the coat having to be sheared off closely.

However, we will assume that the dog is ready to be clipped, and I am going to explain first of all the method of the BASIC CLIP which is the clipping of the face, feet and tail only, for it is with this clip that *all* styles commence. It is the clip that is used for puppies from six weeks old. I will start with the head, and suggest that you study Diagrams 2 and 3. Use your clippers on the hair in the opposite way to which it grows, starting on the right side of the dog's face, clipping slowly and evenly up the side of the cheek. You will find that you have

18

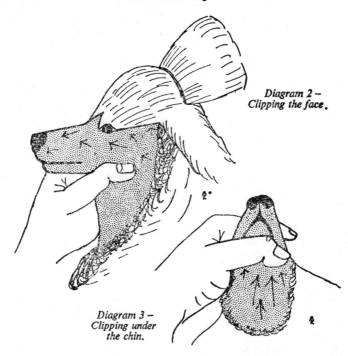

Diagram 2 –
Clipping the face.

Diagram 3 –
Clipping under
the chin.

a better surface for clipping if you slightly pull the skin downwards with your left hand, working your clippers upwards with your right hand.

Now study Diagram 4. There are special lines to be followed on the face and first of all you must aim for a perfectly straight line from the corner of the eye straight across to the ear hole under the ear flap (A to B). The line for the neck should be taken $1\frac{1}{2}''$ to $2''$ below the Adam's apple in the throat, (point C) taken slightly curved up to meet the ear hole again at B. The same procedure should then be followed on the opposite side of the face. Next run your clippers slowly from the stop (point D) down the nose to E, and then on either side

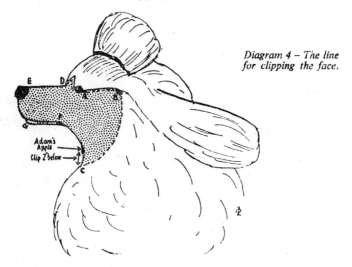

Diagram 4 – The line for clipping the face.

Adam's Apple
Clip 2"below →

of the muzzle, being very careful over the corner of the lip (point F) where one can jag the mouth unless great care is taken. Finally take your clippers from the throat (point C) to the end of the bottom lip (point G). All hair should be clipped from beneath each bottom eye-lid, but it should *never* be clipped off *above* the top eye-lid. If taken off above the top eye-lid it gives the dog a most surprised and ugly expression and is quite incorrect. It is permissible to cut an upside down 'V' up between the eyes. This should be quite narrow, and gives the impression of lengthening the head, and also helps to keep the hair out of the dog's eyes. Finally, go over the face to see if you have missed any parts.

If you are using electric clippers, the bottom blade should overlap the top blade by about one-tenth of an inch, and this should give a very smooth finish. For instance, the Horstman blades need to be adjusted about mid-way, while for the Oster clipper you would use either the No. 10 or No. 15 cutter head,

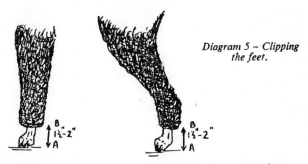

Diagram 5 – Clipping
the feet.

and for the Aesculap you would use the ½ mm. blades.

Next start on the feet, again clipping upwards against the growth of the hair. Clip up to a line 1½" to 2" from the table (point A to B) when the dog is standing (*see Diagram 5*), taking the hair off all round the foot and up this distance towards the ankle. The feet are difficult to clip, as all hair should be completely removed from between the toes, and this can be facilitated by pushing your first and second fingers

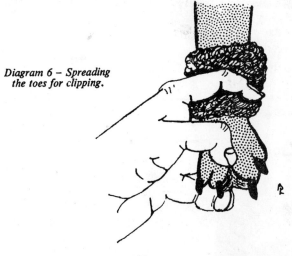

Diagram 6 – Spreading
the toes for clipping.

into the pad underneath the foot, which will automatically cause the dog to spread out his toes, (*see Diagram 6*). If it is impossible to get all the hair removed from between the toes with clippers, the foot should be finished off with a pair of scissors. It is also most important that the hair should be removed from between the pads otherwise if the hair is left it gets caked with mud, etc., and instead of having a nice slim foot, the poodle will have a wide spreading foot. It is easier to do this with scissors than with clippers. When the foot has been neatly clipped, you will find that the longer hair on the leg tends to fall over the foot, and it should then be combed down towards the table, and neatly levelled off all round the ankle, (*Diagram 7*). A poodle seldom enjoys having his feet clipped, and having the intelligence peculiar to the breed he will think up ways of circumventing you. A favourite trick he employs is to lower his head so that his ear fringes get in the way of the clippers. Many poodles have lost their precious ear fringes because of this and a good way to get over the difficulty is put a small nylon cap on him made

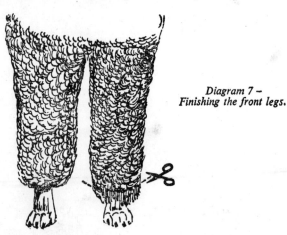

Diagram 7 –
Finishing the front legs.

from a stocking. There is a description of this in Chapter X.

The last part to clip in this basic style is the tail. If your clippers are adjustable, be careful to set them for a *coarser cut* for the tail, for it is here that one can very easily cause a dog to have a 'tickly tail', which will continue to irritate and worry him for days if the hair has been shaved too short – this has often been the reason for a dog losing a prize at a show, as the irritation is intense and he may either carry his tail right over on one side and walk like a crab, or else he may sit down and refuse to walk just at the critical moment – so be warned. The stump of the tail should be clipped from the root up towards the tip for about 1½″ from A to B in Diagram 8.

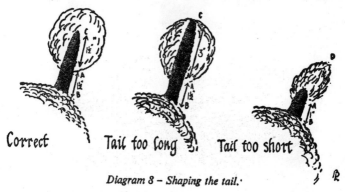

Correct   Tail too long   Tail too short

Diagram 8 – Shaping the tail.

This is if the tail has been originally docked to the correct length, and in this case there will still be about the same length of tail left which is covered by the 'pom' (1½″ from A to C). If, however, a dog has been docked too long, you will still need to clip up for 1½″, but you will find there is still left at least 3″ covered by 'pom', and in this case the long hair of the 'pom' must be cut as close to the end of the stump as possible, (point C). Alternatively the tail may have been docked too short, in which case you should only clip up about an inch, and grow the ' pom ' to extend past the end of the stump for about 3″ (point D). A normal stump of tail on a Miniature should measure approximately 3″, and the end of the ' pom ' should exceed beyond this for a further 1″ to 1½″. It takes quite a time for some poodles to grow a good ' pom ', but it is always advisable to leave as much hair as possible on a puppy's tail to encourage it to grow.

Diagram 8a –
Leaving a moustache.

You have now completed the Basic Clip for any poodle over the age of six weeks old. There is one variation, however, and that is that you may wish to give your poodle a moustache, and if so Diagram 8a will help you. In this case, when clipping the face, you should only clip *half way* from the eye to the end of the nose, leaving the hair round the muzzle long. Some people prefer to leave the hair only on the top lips, clipping clean off from the under jaw right up to the mouth, others like a moustache after the style of a Sealyham or Wire Terrier. It is a matter of personal choice, but it is usually more hygienic if the dog is completely clean shaven, as moustaches are inclined to secrete food and dirt, and so often look untidy and stained.

It now only remains to see that you have not scraped your dog's skin in any place, giving it a tendency to soreness. It is strongly advised that you wipe over all clipped parts either with Johnson's Baby Lotion or Cream, or else (in the case of a white dog), dust liberally with talcum powder. If by any chance a clipper rash does develop, cold cream is a good cure, or a good quality after shaving lotion. But one of the best remedies for a really inflamed clipper rash is to dab on Benzil Benzoate, which will kill any infection and is most soothing. An excellent antiseptic powder is prepared by mixing 20% Zinc Oxide powder with 80% talcum, and sterilising this in a hot oven for an hour. Keep in closed tin and use as required.

If the rash develops, it usually means that you have used the clippers too finely adjusted, or have used them too quickly. The golden rule is always adjust your clippers as wide as will give a good finish, and always make your clipping movements slow and gentle. A much better finish is obtained if the dog has been bathed beforehand, and this also helps to avoid a clipper rash which may be the result of clipping on a dirty skin and laying the pores open to infection.

CHAPTER THREE

The Lion Clip

Measurements and Methods – Shaping of Ruffles
Top-knots – Final Trimming

W E will assume that you have completed the basic clip of
face, feet and tail on your poodle, and are now ready
to start on the Lion Clip.

Lion Clip, or Traditional Clip, is nothing like as difficult
to style as it appears. Diagram 9 shows the relative measurements on a Lion Clip, and the photograph (*Plate 1*) gives an
impression of how your show poodle should look when
completed.

Stage 1. A poodle should have at least 2½" to 3" of coat
before putting him into Lion Clip, and this really should not
be attempted until he is getting on for eight months old. The
first step is to make a very straight parting round the body
at point X in Diagram 10. It is very important to keep this
line well down the poodle's body towards the tail to begin
with, and when you have finally finished the clip you may
find that you can cut the mane a little further up the body
towards the head, when you see the final result of your work.
Comb the mane upwards towards the head from point X, and
downwards towards the tail on the other side of the parting.
In order to keep the mane out of your way while you are
working on the hind quarters, it is quite a good tip to bind
a piece of wide material over the mane from the parting to
above the shoulders. Next rough off with scissors to a length
of approximately 1" all the hair from the parting at X right
down to the ankles at Y.

Diagram 9 – Lion Clip measurement.

Diagram 10 – Commencing the Lion Clip.

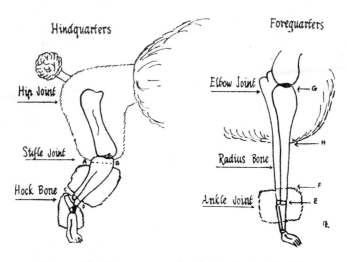

Diagram 11 – Bone structure for shaping legs in Lion Clip.

Stage 2. Now comes the more complicated part of shaping the bands on the hind legs, and the easiest way to accomplish this is to work by feeling the structure of the bones (*see Diagram 11*). A narrow band should be cut in the hair with scissors from point A to B, and this should go right round the leg and should be placed just below the stifle joint. Cut a similar band on the other leg. If you turn your dog with his tail towards you, you should be able to gauge that the lines you have cut are straight and match each other (*see Diagram 12*). Next cut another band from C to D (*Diagram 11*) immediately above the hock bone. This band should slant slightly downwards from C to D. Having satisfied yourself that each pair of bands is quite straight, and that the measurements of both stifle and hock ruffles are approximately those given on Diagram 9, your next job is to clip the bands with the clippers to a depth of approximately $\frac{3}{4}''$.

The Lion Clip

Stage 3. You are now ready to trim the hair on the loins and hips with scissors to a length of about $\frac{3}{4}''$ to 1″. This should be carefully done with the scissors flat against the hair until the coat has the appearance of plush. The quick but rather lazy way to trim the lower back and loins is with clippers set very wide (Oster clipper with No. 5 cutter head, and Aesculap with 7 mm. blades, both used with the clipper going *with* the growth of the hair). But this can never look as nice as when expertly done with scissors. The stifle ruffles (the middle ones) should now be trimmed in like manner but the hair may be left just slightly longer on these. Finally you have the hock ruffles (bottom ones) to trim. Here the procedure is slightly different as the hair should again be a little longer than on the top two ruffles, and to get the real ' snowball ' effect, trimming

Diagram 12 –
Lion Clip viewed
from rear.

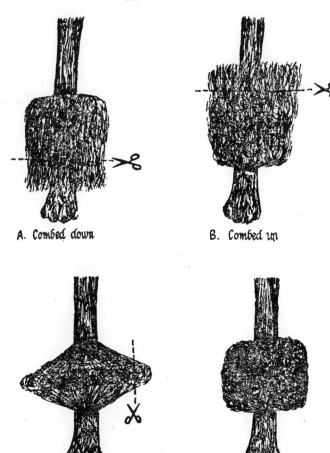

A. Combed down

B. Combed up

C. Combed to middle

D. Completed

Diagram 13 – Trimming anklets (both fore and rear).

should follow three stages, (*see Diagram 13*). 1. Comb the hair of the ruffle down over the foot and then neatly trim round the ends about 1½″ from the ground – point A. Next comb the hair upwards over the band and cut the hair at the top – see point B. Finally comb the hair from the *top* of the ruffle and from the *bottom* until it sticks out round the middle of the ruffle, and trim this off neatly – see point C. Finally trim off any odd ends and this will have produced the smart 'snowball' effect at point D. You now have to round off the hair from the inside of the back legs. Next clip the hair from the belly. It is essential that this should be done with the clippers set as wide as possible, and the skin well powdered afterwards or else dabbed with soothing lotion to prevent any chafing or soreness.

Stage 4. To start on the front legs stand the poodle facing towards you. You will already have clipped the front feet and taken the hair off to about 1½″ from the ground, which you will find is approximately 1″ *below* the ankle joint (*see Diagram 11*). The ankle joint (point E) should come exactly in the middle of the ankle ruffle, therefore carefully make a straight parting in the long hair approximately 1″ *above* the ankle joint (point F). Hold the ankle in your left hand, up to the parting and then with the scissors rough off the long hair up the leg to the elbow joint, (from F to G, under mane). Check that you have a straight line round the leg at point F and then clip the hair off neatly all round the leg up to the actual elbow joint. The hair of the mane will fall rather raggedly over the front legs at point H but we will deal with this later. Repeat the process on the other leg. Now turn to shaping the ankle ruffles, and to do this use exactly the same procedure as described for back ankles and demonstrated in Diagram 13 – A, B, C and D. You should then have really smart rounded ruffles on the front legs.

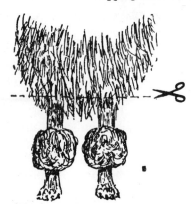

*Diagram 14 – Final
trimming of mane,
front and both sides.*

Stage 5. Now we come to the final trimming of the mane, and you should brush this back from the loins up to the head, neatly trimming off any straggling ends and generally producing the effect of a rounded muff. You will probably find that the hair is straggling over the elbows and below the chest, and the shaping of these parts really adds the final smartness to your poodle. So comb the hair downwards over the elbows and neatly trim off so that about $1\frac{1}{2}''$ to $2''$ of clipped part of front leg is now showing. Turn the poodle to face you and continue the trimming across the lower part of the chest between the front legs, and round the side of the other leg – (*see Diagram 14*).

The shaping and trimming of the tail is dealt with in the preceding chapter.

Final Stage. There now only remains the top-knot to be attended to (*see Diagram 15*). You will already have clipped your poodle's face, and now you must gather up the hair from either side of the forehead and from the back of the head (gather up quite a bit from the back of the head) and slip an elastic band round this. The top ends will probably be a little untidy and uneven, and to get a smart effect you should tip

1. 'Rothara the Roysterer', winner of seven Reserve Challenge Certificates, shown in immaculate Lion Clip.

2. 'Rothara the Courtesan', a Challenge Certificate winner and dam of Int. Ch. Rothara the Gamine and Rothara the Roysterer. Now retired and in Dutch Clip.

3. Drying with hand dryer. Showing dog completely relaxed and Comfortable.

4. *Puppy clip. 'Moss-oaks Yankee Boy' winning son of U.S.A. Champion 'Rothara the Ragamuffin' and owned by Dr and Mrs Wohl of New Orleans U.S.A.*

Photo: Frasie Studio
Chicago

5. *Lamb trim or curly clip. 'Rothara the White Bouquet' demonstrating this style.*

6. *Continental clip. 'Rothara Blanchefontaine Handy Andy', 8½" Toy stud dog, illustrating this clip.*

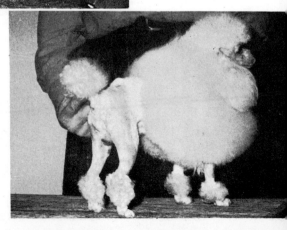

the top of the top-knot just slightly by gathering the hair above the band into the closed fist of your left hand, and cutting off about $\frac{1}{2}''$ of the hair which shows above your hand in a perfectly straight line, and then when released from your hand the top-knot will fan out into a good plume (*see Diagram 15A*). This is done when you have already put an elastic band on the top-knot. There are two ways of wearing the top-knot, you can either take the hair well back from the forehead (*Diagram 15B*) which gives the impression of elongating the head, and also makes for a softer expression which is more suitable for young dogs, or alternatively well forward (*Diagram*

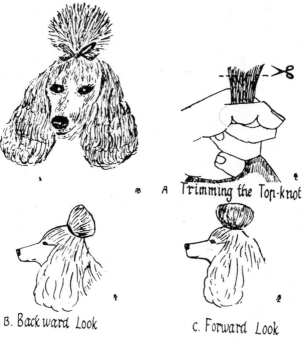

B A Trimming the Top-knot

B. Backward Look

C. Forward Look

Diagram 15 – Top-knots

33

*15*c) which is achieved by drawing the hair forward from the back of the head towards the eyes and then slipping on the rubber band. This gives the poodle an older and more sophisticated look. Either is correct and equally attractive. One final word of warning – don't leave elastic bands on the top-knot for any length of time, or over night, as this splits the hair and you will find your poodle has lost his smart look and has a fringe of ugly whiskers falling over his eyes. Candlewick yarn, which can be purchased in a wide assortment of bright colours for about 1/8d per skein, is excellent for tieing up top-knots as it neither stretches nor shrinks, is soft and yet ties into a tight knot or bow. It is far more satisfactory than wool or ribbon.

You now only have to stand your poodle up, brush his mane upwards at the side and chest and along the back, trim off with the scissors any small taggy ends that spoil the line, and you should have a picture that compares favourably with the poodle in the photograph (*Plate 1*).

CHAPTER FOUR

Dutch Clip or
Modern Trim

Basic Shaping and Measurements
Styling of Shoulder and Hip Pads – Top-knots

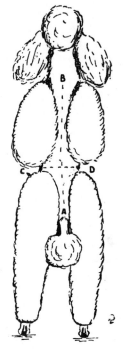

WE assume that you have clipped your poodle in the basic style as already described in Chapter II, and now you wish to put your poodle into Dutch or Modern Trim. Firstly, the coat must be well groomed so that the comb can be taken straight through the hair without encountering any knots or tangles. It will very much enhance the final finish if the poodle is shampooed before clipping and styling.

Stage 1. Study Diagram 16 (bird's eye view) and from this you will see that you must aim at first cutting a cross in the coat. To do this, cut a path with scissors from the root of the tail at A straight up the backbone to point B in the nape of the neck. Next cut a path round the middle of the body as marked C to D on the diagram. The hair in these channels or paths should be cut roughly to about ½″ and should be approximately 1″ wide.

Diagram 16 – Dutch Clip
(bird's eye view).

35

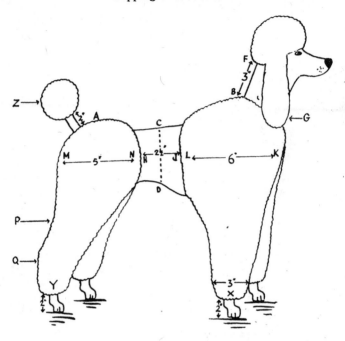

Diagram 17 – Dutch or Modern Clip.

Stage 2. Put a collar loosely round the dog's neck, letting the collar hang rather in the fashion of a loose necklace. Next move to Diagram 17 and clip the hair from the line of the collar (point B) up the back of the neck, to the base of the top-knot at F and round to the basic clip line in front of the neck (point G). Again the hair should be scissored off roughly to about ½″ in length.

Stage 3. You will now see the rough outline of the high shoulder pads and hip pads which are a feature of this particular style. The hair on the short parts of the back (the cross) and

36

on the neck should now be scissored or clipped to an even length of about $\frac{1}{4}''$. The width round body from H to J (*Diagram 17*) should measure approximately $2\frac{1}{2}''$ while the line from A to B (*Diagram 16*) should be about $1\frac{1}{2}''$ wide. The trimming of the short parts takes a little experience, but with practice an expert finish is soon achieved. If you can teach yourself to comb the hair upwards (against the way it grows) and cut the hair with scissors over the top of the comb, you will find this gives an even neater finish. Of course, the quickest and most professional finish for these short parts is done with electric clippers, and to give two examples you would use the No. 5 cutter head (working against the hair) on the Oster Clipper, or the 5 mm. cutter head on the Aesculap Clippers, again cutting against the way the hair grows. But to begin with you may not possess electric clippers and must therefore learn to do the work the longer way with scissors.

Stage 4. Now study Diagram 17 again and you will see that the shoulder pads must be rounded off and shaped so that they are approximately 6″ wide from L to K, tapering down to about 3″ wide at the ankle at point X. The hair should be about 2″ long (or even more) at the top half of the shoulder, diminishing to about 1″ length at the ankle. The hip pads are about 5″ in width M to N, again tapering down to the back ankle, but here the angulation of the back leg should be slightly shown so that the leg is shaped in a little at P and coming outwards again at the hock at Q and then tapering down to point Y. It will be found that the hair on the legs is shaggy and too long. Take the poodle's front leg in your left hand and extend the leg towards you, combing the hair out sideways. Then start cutting the hair from bottom to top of leg all round, widening at the shoulder to meet the large shoulder pad. The same procedure must be followed for shaping the hind leg, and to get a neat and tidy effect the leg should be extended out backwards, the hair combed sideways, trimmed off and tapered to meet the width of hip pad. By this time the hair on all four legs should be even, bushy and springy, and wherever the hair is shorter there should be an impression of plush or thick pile.

Stage 5. For the top-knot, (*see Diagram 18*). There is the round top-knot where the hair is trimmed off all round the head to an even length of about 1″ (*18a*), or alternatively the top-knot can be rounded but left much longer, about 2″ in front (*see 18b*). Either is correct. To get the top-knot really smartly rounded is most difficult – and it is equally difficult to draw an illustration of the method used! but we have attempted to illustrate this in Diagram 18c. First make a parting in the middle of the top-knot on top of the head. Then comb the hair downwards round the head from this central spot. Next take your scissors and neatly snip the hair all round the head to a length of approximately 2″ to 3″. Comb the hair up and slightly backward and you should have a well shaped and rounded top-knot. If it is not quite even trim off roundly to your satisfaction when the hair is combed up. If you wish to taper the hair in a ' V ' at the back of the neck, this can easily be done with the scissors and looks most attractive (*see 18d*). The same method is used for rounding the top of the top-knot in front, but do not round the hair off at the back. Instead comb the hair downwards at the back, cutting a sharp ' V ' at the nape of the neck. The top wings of the ' V ' should reach to the tops of the ears. As the hair goes down to the bottom of the ' V ' it should be tapered shorter and shorter until it mingles in with the very short hair on the neck. Alternatively, the rounded top-knot at the back looks very smart – (*see Diagram 18e*).

Stage 6. Tail: In Dutch or Modern Clip, a profuse and well rounded ' pom ' is often spoilt because the hair has been

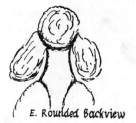

C. Shaping the Top-knot

D. "V" Backview   E. Rounded Backview

Diagram 18 — Top-knots (Dutch Clip).

clipped too far up towards the end of the tail, leaving only a very small area on which to grow the ' pom '. If possible, 2ʺ of the end of the stump of the tail should be left unclipped so that a full and strong ' pom ' may be grown. (*see point Z in Diagram 17 and also Diagram 8*).

Conclusion. For final finish, the ends of the ' trousers ' on all four legs should be neatly trimmed round approximately 2ʺ from the ground. The belly of the poodle should be clipped (not too short or there may occur chafing and soreness), and only with clippers in warm weather. In cold weather, scissors should be used so that hair may be left longer to give protection against chills. On the chest in front, the shoulder pads may merge into one another across the chest, or alternatively a band may be clipped from the throat, down the chest and between the front legs, meeting the clipped belly underneath. Either is correct, but the latter is not recommended in winter or cold weather. A moustache may be left on the muzzle if desired, (*see Diagram 8a*) but it must be borne in mind that whiskers are not very hygienic, since food is picked up in the hair and a moustache thus gets stained and messy. But it is a matter for individual taste. The ear fringes in this style should always be allowed to grow to their natural length and should never be shortened, the longer they grow the better. Hair should never be cut from above the eyes (*i.e.* on forehead). (Please refer to remarks in Chapter II on the Basic Clip.) It is occasionally seen and presumably is done to stop the hair from falling into the eyes, but it is absolutely incorrect and completely spoils the good looks of a poodle. The only thing admissible above the eyes is to cut a small upside down 'V' between the eyes which keeps the hair upright and also gives the impression of elongating the head.

The photograph (*Plate No. 2*) gives an excellent illustration of the Dutch Clip, and was executed most beautifully by Mrs Mary Phillips of Eastcote who trained under the authors. The dog in the photograph is ' Rothara the Courtesan ' who now enjoys a most happy and comfortable life of retirement with Mrs Phillips.

CHAPTER FIVE

Lamb Trim
and Puppy Clip

Advantages of a Short Clip
Use of Comb and Scissors – Age for Clipping Puppies

LAMB TRIM

THIS is a most popular style, and most suitable for companion poodles or brood bitches, or in fact for any poodle which is not being exhibited in the show ring. (*See Plate 5*). It is, perhaps, the easiest clip in which to maintain a poodle, for as the coat is kept to a uniform shortness all over, the dog remains clean and smart at all times, brings in the least amount of mud, or snow, from exercising in bad weather, and is easy to dry if caught in a rain storm, since a quick rub with a rough towel soon restores him again to short tight curls. Also, the poodle can work with the gun in this clip without the bother of brambles clinging to any long hair. Altogether it is a very good utility clip for the poodle who has a job of work to do, and whose main function is not to look a pageant of beauty with all the trimmings! It is a very serviceable clip for the brood bitch while nursing a litter, as the babies' needle claws find little to tangle in her coat while feeding from her and it is easy to clean her up should she become a little messy during the actual whelping. A rub over with a damp cloth which has been wrung out in a weak solution of disinfectant, T.C.P. for instance, will keep her and her little family clean and sanitary during the lactation period – all of which is simple when the coat is in a short Lamb Trim. This clip is sometimes referred to as Curly Clip or Astrakhan Clip, and certainly all three names are equally descriptive.

42

Diagram 19 – Lamb or Curly Trim.

There is not a great deal to describe in the styling of this, in fact three words would suffice – ' cut it short '! But perhaps a few more directions should be given (*see Diagram 19*). As with all styles we are assuming that your poodle has had his basic clip of face, feet and tail as described in Chapter II. Again it is essential to bath the poodle first, and when the coat has been dried with the dryer and well combed out, the hair all over his body should be trimmed off to a length of about ½″. Stand the

Diagram 20 – Curly Clip showing correct angulation.

poodle with his tail towards you, and cut evenly up the back with scissors, round and over the ribs, round the neck, and up to where the top-knot begins at the base of the skull at the back. The underside of the chest and belly is also trimmed short. To get a really smart finish, the hair on both front legs and back legs should remain just a trifle longer, possibly about $\frac{3}{4}''$, and should start with a little added fullness over the buttocks down to the ankle at the back, but still following the bone formation of the hind leg, *i.e.* trimming to show the angulation above the hock bone and the roundness of the stifle joint or patella (*see Diagram 20, Point X*). The added length of coat on front legs commences about half way down the shoulder blade to the wrist, and to get an even roundness on the front legs, turn the dog facing you, hold the leg in your left hand and extend towards you, trimming evenly with the scissors in an upward direction all round, *i.e.* from wrist up to elbow. If you can teach yourself to trim with scissors over the comb, you will find you can get a lovely finish on the coat and with practice this can be made to resemble a really thick plush, but this needs a lot of practice. The comb is pushed into the hair against the way of growth (i.e. from tail to neck), lifted a fraction to give a little more length to the hair you mean to leave on, and then the hair appearing *above* the comb is cut with the scissors. When you become expert at this method you will be able to cut the coat to any length from about $\frac{1}{8}''$ to $3''$, and the finish will be perfectly even with no ridges. One other great advantage is that it obviates any tendency to snip the actual skin of the poodle, as one only snips the metal comb.

The tail in this style usually has the ordinary round pom, and the top-knot follows the style of the Modern or Dutch Clip (*see Diagram 18*). A moustache again is optional.

Undoubtedly, a better and more ' plushy ' finish is obtained in the style with the use of scissors, but of course it does take time. If speed is a great consideration, then the shorter parts of the clip can be done with clippers, but only those makes with a very coarse clipper head can be employed. For instance the Oster Clipper using the No. 5 blade is perfectly adequate, or the Aesculap with the 7 mm. blade. But the longer parts on the legs must be done with scissors otherwise the poodle looks most odd with skin tight legs. Where the clipped body hair and the longer hair meet, this must be carefully tapered in with use of scissors over a comb to obviate a noticeable difference in length of cut.

PUPPY CLIP

A most enchanting style and generally used for all puppies up to about eight or nine months old, when they will be put into one of the more mature styles. It is difficult to describe this style in detail since it emerges gradually from the time the puppy is about six weeks old. Most puppies have the basic clip of face, feet and tail about the time they leave their mothers or when they are sold and go out into the world. At this age

Diagram 21 –
Puppy hair style.

nothing more is done to the coat, but as they grow older straggly wispy ends begin to appear, and the coat should then be tipped all over at intervals of about six weeks until ready for an adult clip. We suggest you turn to the photograph (*Plate 4*) showing a puppy in show puppy clip, and you will see from this that the coat has been tipped and rounded off to look very smart. The hair should be left as long as possible only just taking off the straggling tips, since you will, in the case of a show puppy, need all the coat available for mane, anklets, ruffles, etc. for his graduation into the Lion Clip. Again a slight shaping inwards is given on the hind legs above the hock to show angulation, and also the coat is cut at the bottom of the ribs near the elbow in an upward direction towards the point where the hind leg meets the last rib – this is particularly noticeable in the photograph of the Puppy Clip. The hair at the tail end of the backbone should be so shaped, that when the tail is held up in the normal manner, the coat is well clear of this. If the hair is left so that it meets the upstanding tail, this will give the impression of a long back. It makes a great difference to the look of the poodle puppy when the hair is trimmed up the back from the tail for a couple of inches in a gradual manner.

Most show puppies wear a slide to keep the top-knot back (*see Diagram 21*), or else the hair is left long and just brushed or combed up. The usual Lion Clip top-knot is rather too mature and sophisticated for the young puppy. For the companion puppy, very often the top-knot is shaped into a round as in Lamb or Dutch Clip as it grows longer, and this is very sensible as otherwise the hair falls over the face and gets in the puppy's eyes, and there is really little advantage in keeping the top-knot long unless the puppy is destined for the show ring. But however you decide to control the top-knot, with slides, rubber bands, ribbons or wool, do only leave such things on the head for a little while at a time and never throughout the night. The puppy hair is soft and breaks easily, and if bands or suchlike are left on for any length of time, you will soon find the top-knot has degenerated into a few wisps. To grow a really lengthy and dense young adult coat, it pays to tip the puppy coat at about four to five months of age.

One last word about puppy clipping. Puppies are usually cutting their second teeth at about four to five months old, and this is a time when they need particularly gentle and careful handling. It is often found that at this time it becomes well nigh impossible to clip a puppy's face. It will pay you to leave the clipping process for a week or two until the new teeth are through. It is a bad time for him and his whole face and mouth may be very sore. If he is hurt at this time, although it may be quite unintentional on your part, it may make him jumpy for ever after. It pays to go very carefully when you see the little baby teeth beginning to get loose. Equally it is essential to start clipping a puppy when he is really young – six weeks is not a bit too early and keep clipping him regularly. The puppy who is left ' rough ' until six or seven months sometimes completely refuses to have either scissors or clippers anywhere near him – and the ensuing battle shatters both his and your nerves and you will probably at that moment wonder why you didn't buy a smooth Dachshund or a Bull Terrier! But the puppy who starts his clipping experience at six weeks is seldom any trouble and takes it all in the normal day's work.

Don't leave a collar on your show puppy for any length of time as this again rubs off the hair very quickly. Whether you have a show puppy or one as a companion, don't clip him for too long at a time. Clip one part of him, then let him have a run round and give him something to play with. Then clip a little more for a few minutes. He will be quite interested if the experience only lasts for a few minutes at a time, but if it goes on too long he will become bored and restless and thoroughly play you up, and as a result will come to dread the clipping days. The results of your gentleness and consideration for a puppy will be manifested usually in a willing and co-operative adult poodle who really enjoys his titivating.

CHAPTER SIX

Various Other Clips

Second Puppy Clip – Continental Clip
Belgian Clip

THERE are three main variations to the popular styles already described, and while not in general use they are seen from time to time, both in the Show ring and on the companion poodle.

SECOND PUPPY CLIP

This is a variation of the Puppy Clip and is used for older puppies in the Show ring generally between the ages of nine and twelve months, (*see Diagram 22*). In this clip the front half of the poodle is in Lion Clip, that is to say the front legs are clipped and ruffles shaped on the ankles, the top-knot and mane are cut and styled as in Lion Clip. But the back half of the poodle, from the end of the mane, is left without any shaping as in the orthodox Puppy Clip. Thus, the tail is clipped

Diagram 22 – Second puppy clip.

with the ' pom ' on the end, and the hair is left on the back legs at a length of about one inch from loin down to ankle, with no shaping of bands on the legs but with the feet clipped in the usual manner. This is really an intermediate clip which combines half Puppy Clip and half Lion Clip.

CONTINENTAL CLIP

Then there is the Continental Clip, and as its name implies this is used mostly on the Continent and rarely seen in England (*see Plate 6*). In this clip the hindquarters of the poodle are closely shaved from the ankle ruffle right up over the thighs and loins to the beginning of the mane. The mane is cut a little higher (that is about an inch further up the body towards the head) and the length of the mane is rather shorter and closer than in the Lion Clip. In this clip the top-knot is not usually tied up in a ' pom ', but is left loose and brushed upwards, somewhat like the top-knot in Modern Clip but rather longer. A very brief moustache is sometimes left on the upper lips of the muzzle, but it is equally correct for the poodle to be clean shaven. Various decorations may be styled on the hips and the most usual is a round pom of hair about $\frac{3}{4}''$ to 1 '' long cut out on either side of the lower loin. Sometimes this decoration is cut into the form of a heart on either side, or a ring with the centre cut out, and depends really on how expert you are with the scissors or clippers and how your fancy takes you! It is difficult to get the two poms or rings exactly equal in size and the best way to do this is to hold a tumbler (or wine glass) against the hair on the lions before clipping right down, and snip the hair round the edge of the glass. This will give you the line for a perfect round, and having snipped out this circle on both sides, you then clip the rest of the back legs of the poodle. The two ' poms ' can then be trimmed off to an even length. Another form of decoration is to leave a ring of hair round the base of the tail about 1 '' wide and ¾" long, but I do not think this is as elegant as the two ' poms '. It is not advisable to put a poodle into Continental Clip unless you are absolutely sure he is sound in the hind-quarters as it is a most revealing clip and shows up every defect in bone structure. But if the hind legs are well angulated, and well muscled and perfect in structure, then this clip can look most attractive. Maybe it suits the large Standard poodle better than the Miniature or Toy, but this is probably a matter of opinion. This clip should not be adopted for the first time in cold weather, as it certainly exposes the dog's kidneys to chill, and undoubtedly is more suited as a hot weather style.

BELGIAN CLIP

The final variation is the Belgian Clip, so called because so

Diagram 23 – Belgian Clip.

many poodles are seen in this style in Belgium (*see Diagram 23*). Here the body is clipped moderately short to a length of about ½",but the hair on the front legs from the lower shoulder down to the ankle, and that on the back legs from lower hip to ankle is left long, about 2". The hair round the neck is clipped short, and the top-knot is shaped into a small round cap, rather giving the impression of sitting on top of the head. The hair on the ears is clipped quite short with the exception of the bottom few hairs of the fringe which are left about 1" to

Diagram 24 – Head style for Belgian or Kerry Clip.

1½" long (*see Diagram 24*). The tail is clipped short with no ' pom ', and the feet and face are clipped short in the ordinary way. Usually a small moustache is worn, but this is optional. There seems little to commend this Clip either from beauty or usefulness, but some owners favour it. It is sometimes referred to as the ' Kerry Clip ' and certainly is a slight copy of the Kerry Blue Terrier trim.

CHAPTER SEVEN

Shampooing and Drying

Preparation of Bath – Temperature of Water
Selection of Shampoo – Drying – A Control Gadget

To make the best of your poodle it is really essential that he should be shampooed *before* clipping. For one thing, it is much easier to clip the hair into any style when it is clean and upstanding, and for another it gives a glossy and well conditioned finish to the poodle. But a very special word of warning here – do not attempt to shampoo a poodle unless he is completely free of knots and tangles. This is absolutely essential, for if he is bathed when he is still knotty, these tangles will then form into a thick felt which it is well nigh impossible to free, and it is then only possible to clip the poodle's coat close to the skin and say goodbye to all one's aspirations to a smart clip for the time being. So be careful to comb right through from head to tail, teasing out with your fingers any knots and tangles there are. Next, give your poodle a short rest after the energy of grooming, and prepare everything ready for the bath. Dilute the shampoo in a beaker of hot water, put the towel and the dryer ready, have the spray ready fixed on the taps and be sure the water is hot, and will remain hot, until you have finished rinsing the poodle. Place a piece of rubber matting in the bottom of the sink to prevent the poodle from slipping about and see that there is nothing on the side of the sink or bath which can rattle down and frighten him in any way. Next, plug his ears with cotton wool, for water seeping down into the ear probably causes more ear trouble than anything else. It is possible to buy *non-*absorbent cotton wool for this purpose. Use only *one* piece of wool in the ear and press firmly and securely down into the ear, and don't forget to remove the swab when the bath is over. Another word of warning here. Always be careful to test the heat of the water. This should be just a little warmer than blood heat, and if you test this either with your own elbow or inside of wrist you will soon know the right temperature. It must be a terrible sensation to a dog to have too hot water played on him and be unable to get away from it. Equally cold water shocks him and may well give him a chill. The same applies to the hot air from a dryer. Be careful to constantly check this throughout the drying process and do not hold the nozzle of the dryer too close to his skin.

Next, stand the dog in the sink and wet him all over, squeezing the coat to ensure that he is wet to the roots – there is nothing more waterproof than a poodle's coat. When thoroughly wet, pour a little of the shampoo on the coat from shoulder to tail and massage into a thick lather. Lather each leg in turn and finally the head and ears. Rinse off with the spray, and then use the remainder of the shampoo for a second quick lather all over. Then finally rinse well until no shampoo remains in the coat. Squeeze all surplus water from the coat, and dry the poodle's face with a towel. Let him shake if he wants to, in fact it helps if you train him to do this on the word ' shake '. Wrap him in a thick towel and take him to the table for drying.

DRYING: A good brisk rub with the towel and then start to dry him with the dryer. To get a really smart finish, you should first brush the hair while blowing the hot air through the coat, and then use the dryer while you comb through the hair systematically all over the poodle. You will find it a great help if you train your poodle to lie on each side in turn for this dry-and-comb operation as you can then easily dry his tummy, chest and insides of back legs. Put a pad of towel under his head and he will usually drop off to sleep if he really is comfortable, and this simplifies your task (*see Plate 3*). Also train yourself to manipulate the dryer in your left hand so that you can brush and comb with your right hand – quite a difficult feat!

Diagram 25 - Hair dryer on metal stand, freeing both hands for holding.

A very good gadget is a ' stand ' made especially for hand dryers and obtainable for about 6/-. The dryer can be supported on the stand, thus freeing one of your hands, and this greatly helps in drying puppies or restive dogs. This stand is shown in Diagram 25.

A supply of good quality towels, of the type that really soak up the wet, is essential, and there are usually some available from the household which are rather old and these come in very well for ' Dog Towels '. A cork bath mat is another ' must ' when shampooing. These mats soak up the wet and the dog can be laid on the table for the drying process without lying in a pool of water. They cost about 10/- to 12/- to buy.

If you possess an infra-red lamp, this can be used most successfully for the drying of puppies, or adult dogs with short coats, for that matter. If the dog is placed on towels in an upturned tea chest with the lamp hung at a suitable distance above the box, he will dry quite quickly. Be careful here – the temperature on the back of the damp poodle should not exceed 70° - 80° F. and a thermometer should be fixed in the box at the height of the dog's back or head. A piece of wire netting or a wire frame on top of the box obviates the puppy or dog climbing out.

You may well find your poodle is inclined to sit or lie down when you wish him to stand up so that you can dry his legs, and in this case some sort of support may be necessary to get him to co-operate (*see Diagram 26*). We have used this type of ' sling ' for years and it is quite simple to make. Have a fairly wide scarf with each end gathered into a large curtain pin. From a hook in the ceiling above your drying table, hang a chain with another hook on the end. Put the sling round the poodle's middle and hang the curtain pins on the hook. Adjust the chain to the right height to support him without stringing him up. This will make him very comfortable and relaxed and you will be able to dry his legs, chest, head and ears without any difficulty.

After shampooing is the time to cut a poodle's nails, as they are then soft and pliable and easy to cut. Do be careful not to let your poodle out into cold air outside until at least two to three hours after bathing. Also he should not be fed within two hours either way, of bathing, and don't forget to let him relieve himself before you put him in the tub.

If your poodle has the misfortune to pick up either some fleas, lice or ticks, bathing in a gammexane solution will rid him of such pests. Two tablespoonsful of gammexane powder

Diagram 26 – Sling control.

stirred into a gallon of warm water, and sponged over the poodle for five minutes is usually successful. This should be repeated in five days' time. Do not rinse off the solution, but dry immediately with the dryer.

For anything more serious and tenacious, such as a parasitic skin trouble or a mild form of Kennel mange, a cure can usually be effected by shampooing in ' Seleen ' manufactured by Abbotts Ltd. The directions must be most carefully followed as the solution is very strong and it is wiser to ask your Vet's advice first.

57

SHAMPOOS: Of all canine breeds, the poodle coat requires very special care in the selection of the correct type of shampoo to be used, and to imagine that any shampoo is ' good enough for a dog ', especially the poodle, is indeed very bad policy, besides being most uneconomic. Most careful consideration must be given to your choice of shampoo, otherwise the result certainly will be very disappointing, as the poodle's coat is of a wooly texture, and he does not shed it as other dogs do. Therefore when his bath has been completed, the coat must be left ' tangle free ' allowing air to circulate through easily and the pores to breathe freely.

One of the primary causes of a dowdy coat is the indiscriminate use of harsh shampoos, which assuredly produce disastrous results, not only to the coat, but to the unfortunate dog itself, whose skin is far more sensitive than that of the human, and must be treated as such. Moreover when the coat takes on a dull lifeless appearance, scurf and dandruff are usually present, and the poor animal is worried to death with incessant scratching, accompanied by a pronounced display of restlessness, which in turn adversely affects the general health.

Tolerance of these conditions is by no means complimentary to the owner, in whose hands the remedy lies to put these matters right with the special preparation most suitable for the job in hand. The incorrect choice of shampoo for your poodle, simply invites disaster to the beautiful coat that these lovely animals can, and should carry, for with their use the hair shafts become harsh and brittle, break, and eventually lose all flexibility and wither, leaving thin patches with a sparse general appearance.

One of the greatest disadvantages of shampooing with unsuitable preparations, is the deposition of lime scum that has been put back into the coat in the form of a sticky curd, acting as an adhesive, and creating acute ' tangle '. This scum, when dry, becomes fine dust (sometimes wrongly mistaken for dandruff) which not only clogs the pores of the skin, but settles as an opaque film on each hair shaft, giving complete dullness.

To assume that any type of shampoo selected for a White poodle, will successfully shampoo say a Black, would be inviting great disappointment. In the case of the White poodle, the particular type of shampoo designed for this colour should be obtained. This shampooing should be carried out as near the show date or special function as possible, so that the dazzling white, and harsh springy texture of the coat is preserved to the last minute. When the shampoo has been completed, and while the coat is still wet, 'Cream Coat Corrector' should be applied, by gently massaging right through the coat, and then rinsing out with a spray. This cream will automatically neutralize all lather and lime scum, and its high lanoline content will ensure that a greater part of the natural oils lost in the process of shampooing are adequately replaced, in addition to taking complete care of the removal of 'Tangle'.

Shampooing the Black poodle again needs care in the choice of the correct type designed for this particular colour, otherwise a 'slatey' black is the result. Specialised shampoos for Black poodles are obtainable which enhance the polished ebony look of an immaculate coat that is so much desired. Best results are obtained from this specialised shampoo, by washing the poodle about three or four days before you wish him to look his best. This ensures that the coat is scrupulously clean, and leaves a few days interval to complete the grooming by intermittent brisk brushing to develop a rich sheen and bloom, without the use of any artificial lubricants.

Many owners tell us with pride that they only use the best shampoos obtainable for human hair, and excellent as they are for the purpose for which they are intended, they are not good for a poodle's coat. The chief aim of such shampoos is to make the hair silky and soft, and just the reverse is required in the poodle, where the coat should be bushy and springy and of a rather harsh texture – anything in the nature of silky or soft is counted a fault.

There are, of course, many makes of dog shampoos which are good, but we very much doubt whether any manufacturer has put in so many years of real hard research and work to produce the ideal shampoo for the poodle as Mr Charles Warren of 'Vitacoat' Ltd. He has been for a great many years connected with the hairdressing profession and there is no doubt that practically all the well known poodle breeders and exhibitors use his 'Vitacoat' preparations. After all, if you own a poodle, presumably you like the spectacle of one that is beautifully put down, and want your own particular poodle to look the same. We feel convinced this can only be achieved by using the right preparation for the right dog. Mr Warren has evolved such shampoos as 'Bleu Foncé' for Whites and Creams, 'Charbon' for Blacks or Blues, 'Sylversheen' for Silvers, 'Lemonegg' for all coloured poodles except Whites, and a most excellent general all-purpose shampoo in 'Antiscurf'. He has given special attention to the development of treatment shampoos which counter the disadvantages of dry coats, also to the alleviation of scurf and dandruff, not leaving out the necessity of a shampoo sometimes required for the removal of livestock. Brittle coats can be corrected by the use of special oil shampoos designed for this purpose, whilst there are shampoos incorporating coconut oil, that will nourish a 'tatty' coat back to a healthy condition. Another preparation to be recommended is 'Quikleen' the spirit shampoo which requires no water.

For use in a Beauty Parlour as a coat spray which gives a finish to the coat with a nice fragrant smell, is 'Vitacoat Eleganza'. Most of these shampoos and tonics are not expensive and can be obtained through all good chemists or else direct from ' Vitacoat ' Ltd, 30 Upland Road, South Croydon. I believe I am right in saying that the Royal dogs are regularly shampooed with ' Vitacoat ' when attending the famous Beauty Parlour in Beauchamp Place owned by Colonel Beddoes. Anyway, if you want to know more about these special poodle shampoos send to Mr Warren for more details.

If you are running a Beauty Parlour it is a good idea to stock some of these special shampoos, rinses and conditioners. You should charge extra for their application, and will be quite safe in doing so as they are made from good quality ingredients, and will definitely improve the dog's coat.

CHAPTER EIGHT

The Poodle Beauty Parlour

Cleanliness – Gentle Handling – Insurance – Scale of Charges

WE would like to make it clear that the next two chapters are not really intended for the novice owner breeder, but for those who plan to set up their own Poodle Beauty Parlours, and therefore the matter it contains may be slightly technical.

Month by month more and more poodles come to the Beauty Parlours for attention. A great majority of them are good poodles with profuse springy coats, good conformation and condition, and co-operative jolly temperaments. But also there come the bad poodles – those with open straggling coats, nervously thin and in poor condition, and with mean and spiteful natures. Those in the first category give us a good deal of pleasure to clip and we revel in turning them out into smart and jaunty specimens of a grand breed. But the second category gives us many problems as so often the coats are too thin, straggling and dull to look smart in any clip. Also because of their doubtful temperaments they do not take kindly to handling by strangers. And here we must take every precaution for our own hands for they are our livelihood and we cannot afford to be bitten. If a dog shows signs of biting then it is wise to put a bandage round the muzzle, and while it would not altogether prevent him from biting, it at least gives one time to get out of reach. If a dog is very nervous and frightened on coming to the Beauty Parlour, an Asprin will often calm his nerves and allow him to take the ordeal in his stride, and one Asprin cannot harm him. Anything stronger in the way of a tranquiliser or sedative should never be given

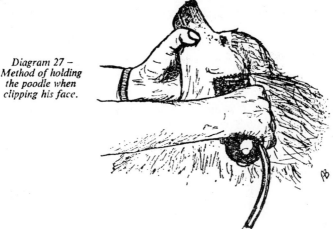

*Diagram 27 –
Method of holding
the poodle when
clipping his face.*

except on the instructions of a qualified Vet. But, and I cannot stress this too much, gentle handling will do more than anything else to make the poodle tractable, and caressing hands and a gentle voice will nearly always completely reassure the normal poodle when he comes to be clipped. Move slowly, talk quietly to him, put him on the table gently and start with the parts he minds least. Always have him on a lead fixed to the wall behind the table as a dog can make a sudden rush so quickly and fall off the table, and with such fine bones, a fracture occurs almost without warning.

It is essential when taking in dogs for attention that your premises are spotless, and easily disinfected. Instruments such as scissors, combs, brushes, etc., must be regularly disinfected. If you can have a tiled floor so much the better as this can be mopped over with disinfectant frequently. If not, the next best thing is linoleum, but water tends to seep under this in the corners. Tables should be covered with either lino or Formica, which again can be well swabbed.

Rubber mats from Woolworth's are excellent on the table to prevent the dog from skidding, and these can be washed in disinfectant.

Combs and scissors, tooth scrapers and nail clippers should be disinfected after each customer, and thoroughly boiled from time to time. Wash your own hands frequently and also wear clean aprons or coats. A customer has a right to expect that all reasonable precautions are taken to ensure that his dog does not pick up any disease in your Beauty Parlour, or take away with him any parasites left as a gift from the previous customer.

We would strongly advise that you go into the matter of Insurance, for it must be remembered that in handling other people's animals a certain responsibility rests with the owner of a Beauty Parlour and, whatever precautions are taken, there is always the possibility that an animal may be accidently injured. It is possible that the owner might bring a claim against the Beauty Parlour and some owners have very fanciful ideas of the value of their pets.

Some people are difficult to reason with and the really awkward ones are liable to dash off to a solicitor and threaten proceedings, feeling that the Beauty Parlour could not afford to fight a claim owing to the bad publicity. This is a risk that can be insured against at a very reasonable premium and a policy to cover such contingencies is available through the Dog Breeders' Insurance Co Ltd of Beacon House, Lansdown, Bournemouth, or The Canine Insurance Association Ltd, of 1 Gracechurch Street, London, E.C.3, both of whom specialise in Dog Insurance. Effecting such a Policy is a very wise precaution and is, in fact, ' paying for peace of mind ' as when there is trouble, this becomes the Insurance Company's worry.

There is also the possibility that an animal in the care of a Beauty Parlour may cause damage or injury to a third party and a claim may be made. This is covered by a general Third

7. *Puppy Face clipping. Showing one with moustache left on, and the other clean shaven.*

(right) Control frame. The frame is securely screwed to the grooming table, and completely controls the dog.

Photo: Margaret Worth

9. *Mrs. Rothery Sheldon receiving the Best in Show Cup from the Duke of Bedford at Bedford Show when the white miniature Poodle 'Rothara the Roysterer' gained the top award in an entry of 1,630.*

Cruft's dog show. A string of Rothara Miniature Poodle Stud dogs benched at world's greatest show.

Photo: Margaret Worth

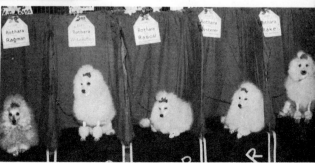

11. Mrs. Rothery Sheldon (right) and Miss Barbara Lockwood with Claude (Rothara the Tympany of Tusette) at Kingfisher's Reach.

12. American show clip, U.S.A. Champion Rothaara the Ragamuffin winning the Supreme Award, handled by Mr. Larry Downey, and immaculately prepared.

Photo: Frasie Studio Chicago

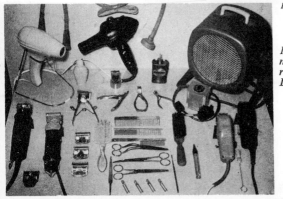

13 Beauty Parlour Equipment. Most of the items required in a flourishing Beauty Parlour.

Party Policy if this extends to cover animals not only owned by the insured but also temporarily in their custody and care.

What would seem more likely is that an animal receiving beauty treatment might bite one of the assistants. This would not come within the scope of Third Party Insurance, as an assistant would not be considered a third party. A claim can be made under National Health Insurance for injuries sustained whilst at work, but in the event of an assistant receiving severe injuries – and a comparatively minor attack upon a girl's face might cause a permanent disfigurement – a claim can be made against the employer under Common Law. Here again, the risk can be covered by an Insurance Policy at quite a nominal premium.

When first setting up to clip poodles it may surprise you to discover how many poodles are brought to you in a really shocking condition. When you are welcoming a new customer, take the precaution of examining the poodle's coat before quoting a fee for the services required, because although in these days of modern clippers it is possible to clip off a matted coat, there is no doubt that it will take a great deal longer than it does to clip the poodle who is well groomed and cared for, and you must charge accordingly. After all, you can probably clip two well cared for poodles in the time it takes you to get the mats and tangles out of one. Also this may inspire the owner to keep the dog in better condition thereafter.

Another point, make sure the owner has allowed the poodle to relieve himself before coming to be clipped, because nothing makes a dog more restless and jumpy than if he has not had the opportunity. If the dog is to have a heavy coat clipped right down and the weather is chilly, ask the owner to bring a dog coat with him – or else keep one or two by you, so that you can lend these out when necessary. It is so easy for a dog to catch a chill after bathing and clipping – and you will be held responsible!

A most valuable addition to the Beauty Parlour is a set of large photographs, drawings or diagrams showing the various poodle styles. So many owners do not quite know what style they want, and such pictures will make it quite clear, obviating any confusion as to what clip the poodle was expected to have.

An important matter is the planning of your price list, and here I would stress that you decide on the prices you are going to charge and *stick to them*. A fatal mistake is to charge Mrs So-and-So less because she happens to be a friend of a friend, etc. It very soon gets round that you charge less to some and more to others, and this will definitely embarrass you. Another point, try to work out your charges correctly at the beginning and do not fall into the error of being too cheap. It is difficult to raise your charges and yet it is very easy to forget when your Beauty Parlour is an exciting dream that you may soon have to pay an assistant, that you may need a lot more equipment, that you may need another room, that all the electrically powered equipment brings in an extra Electricity Board account, that you may need a telephone or the calls on your existing 'phone may be doubled or trebled. You are apt to forget these things and may then suddenly realise that you are not charging enough to make a reasonable profit. On page 67 is a suggested scale of charges on which to base your prices. It is worth while having a price list printed so that there can be no argument! On the reverse side it is quite an idea to have an appointment card to give to your clients so that they will not forget when they have fixed to come again.

To begin with, a small advert. in your local paper under the ' Dog ' or ' Livestock ' column will bring you your first customers, and it is better to have this in say for four weeks at a time so that dog owners get used to seeing it and know where to look for it. One insertion is rather inclined to be lost and never seen again.

SUGGESTED SCALE OF CHARGES FOR CLIPPING, SHAMPOOING, ETC.

Cutting out first time in Lion Clip (including shampoo)	.....	.....	from 35/- to	45/-
Cutting out first time in Dutch or Modern Clip (including shampoo)	.....		,, 30/- to	40/-
Cutting out first time in Lamb or Curly Trim (including shampoo)	.....		,, 25/- to	35/-
Maintenance Clipping from existing styles	.....		,, 15/- to	25/-
Ditto, but including shampoo	.....	.....	,, 20/- to	30/-
Puppy Clipping (face, feet and tail)	.....	.....	,, 7/6 to	12/6
Ditto, but including shampoo	.....	.....	,, 12/6 to	20/-
Teeth Cleaning and Nail Cutting	.....	.....	,, 5/- to	7/6
Show Preparation, including shampoo, Clipping, Teeth and Nails		.....	,, 30/- to	50/-
Shampooing only according to condition of coat and size of dog		.....	,, 7/6 to	15/-
Special Coat Conditioners, Rinses, Treatments, etc.			,, 7/6 to	15/-
Contract Clipping, which is once every month or six weeks for twelve months, payable quarterly or yearly, and which includes a shampoo every two months, clipping and care of nails and teeth			,, 8 to 14 gns.	

Extra charges for coats that are matted or for very difficult dogs which take a longer time, on the basis of 3/6 to 7/6 per hour extra to above charges.

Note. *These prices apply to England only, and would possibly be quite different in other countries.*

But the thing to remember is that the success of your Beauty Parlour will be built up entirely on personal recommendation, therefore the more customers' poodles enjoy coming to you and the more you can clip them without frightening or upsetting them, the more business you are going to build up.

Don't let inexperienced learners practise on your customers' dogs, and keep a sharp eye on how your assistants handle the dogs. Any roughness or loss of temper must be forbidden, and however good an assistant may be technically and artistically, if she ' takes it out of the dogs ' she is worse than useless to you. Equally the girl who is indefinite and sentimental will never get the job done. It is the happy medium one wants in the girl who is firm, efficient and businesslike and yet who really loves dogs and thinks ahead for their welfare, and will go to endless trouble to make it easier and less upsetting for the dog. After all, it *is* upsetting to a little poodle, at any rate the first time he is left alone with a stranger, and has all these things done to him, and he needs all the gentleness and reassurance you can possibly give him so that he will not mind a return visit. Your reputation rests on the report the poodles give of *you* when they return to their owners.

One final point, don't accept appointments to put poodles into difficult and unusual clips until you have learnt how to do it. It is easy to make a mess of a difficult clip the first time you attempt it. Try it out on your own poodles first, or persuade your friends to let you practice on their dogs free of charge for the experience, and if you are doubtful of the result at first, ask the opinion of a first class breeder or exhibitor. They will tell you if you have made a creditable job of it and usually do not mind being asked for advice. So pocket your pride and ask – it is much better than making a hash of a customer's dog and you will so quickly learn to be proficient.

CHAPTER NINE

Equipment for the
Beauty Parlour

Choice of Equipment – Prices of Equipment – Control Frame –
Measures and Measuring

You will need a certain amount of equipment when you start your Beauty Parlour, and in this chapter we have tried to give you a good description of the items that are really necessary. It is so easy to pay dearly for experience, buying many things which sound useful but turn out to be unsuitable for the job. Although some of the items are expensive, it must be remembered that no business can be started without a small amount of capital, and there is no doubt the number of poodles who need clipping are legion and if you can do the job efficiently you will soon collect all the customers you need and quickly pay for the necessary equipment. But equally, so many gadgets can be built up as you go along and as business progresses. You can do so much with a little ingenuity and imagination. For instance, a couple of small indoor kennels or even travelling boxes are very useful in which to pop a poodle while he is waiting his turn or awaiting collection. Also a couple of rings screwed to the wainscoting on which to tie a lead are very handy for the waiting poodle – a light chain is better as leads can always be chewed through. A clinical thermometer is an essential as, although one cannot always decide if a dog is ill or sickening, any dog whose coat is dull, whose eye is heavy, and whose general appearance is dejected is one who should be suspect, and you will be on the safe side to check that his temperature is not more than one degree higher or lower than the normal

101.5°. Any dog who is suspect, and running even a slight temperature should be refused. You owe it to your other customers to take this precaution.

But now let's turn to the actual equipment needed, and study the best makes and types of what is required.

SCISSORS: We have sought guidance from the Diamond Edge Company and cannot do better than quote their sound advice, and we personally have always found the scissors we have purchased from this Company to be first class and completely reliable. The preference they give is for German made scissors. The reason for this is that the Germans have specialised to a considerable extent in these scissors and in doing so have introduced a very high quality steel into the blades which, in our experience, holds its edge much longer

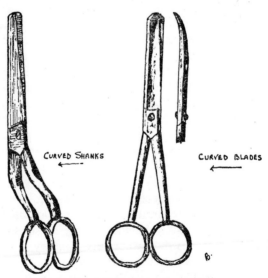

CURVED SHANKS ←

CURVED BLADES ←

Diagram 28 – An example of curved blade scissors, and those with curved shanks.

70

than scissors made in France or Sheffield. This does not mean to say that some scissors made in Sheffield are not good quality, but on the whole we have found the German ones the better ' buy '. Some of the scissors made in France are very good, but generally our experience is that the quality of steel, or possibly the tempering methods employed, leave the steel of the blade relatively a little softer than the steel of the German manufactured scissors. Quite a number of breeders and exhibitors use scissors of poor quality steel and in fact some are cold forged, and it cannot be expected to get a good and lasting use from such scissors. Therefore it really pays to buy good ones in the beginning. We would suggest that you buy 6½″ or 7″ Diamond Edge Special or de Luxe, and these cost about 15/- to 17/6d. a pair. You will also find a pair of curved blade scissors invaluable for trimming the short parts of the poodle and these can be bought from Diamond Edge for 10/6d (6″) or 12/6d (7″). (*See Diagram* 28).

NAIL CLIPPERS: We have found the Guillotine type the most suitable for poodles, and certainly poodles object to these far less than to the ordinary nippers. These can be purchased for 19/6d a pair, while the nail nippers go from about 9/- to 17/6d a pair according to size.

COMBS: When choosing trimming combs, it is essential to ask for a brass comb with steel pins coated with chromium. These can be boiled or washed in disinfectant satisfactorily but the nickel ones do not wear so well and are inclined to bend, and also the metal peels off leaving scratchy edges. A comb with a handle is good for coarse work, while a comb with one end coarse and the other end fine is excellent for finishing work. These can be purchased from about 5/- to 8/-, and we have always obtained ours from Messrs Spratts Ltd, 41 Bow Road, London E.1.

BRUSHES: Everyone seems to have a different opinion on this subject and the ideal brush is hard to find. We have been faithful for many years to the ordinary ' Addis ' Nylon hair brush used by humans 'and priced at 8/11d. These last well, wash very easily and keep the poodle's hair in excellent condition. There are many other types on the market – whalebone, those with bristles set in rubber cushions, wire brushes, etc, and it is a matter for individual preference.

CLIPPERS: If you intend to clip professionally it is essential to have at least one pair of electric clippers. There are now quite a number of these on the market and we have worked with Oster, Aesculap, Forfex, Clukés and Horstman and all have their good points. Again we have asked the Diamond Edge Company for their technical advice and they tell us that their experience over the last few months shows that the Oster has now taken first place in their sales of electric clippers for poodle clipping, being followed by the Aesculap and next by the Forfex. The Horstman is not powered by an electric motor and therefore does not have the power of the other three. It has its limitations and cannot be expected to cope with rough work, but for the owner breeder with a few dogs we cannot stress strongly enough that we think the Horstman clipper (*illustrated in Diagram 1*) is excellent for private work; but for the Beauty Parlour one of the high powered makes is essential.

After considerable testing we have chosen the Oster as being the best clipper on the market. The blades are easily changed (just one small screw) and there seems to be less danger of snagging or cutting the dog when using these. The No. 5 blade will shear off a badly matted coat, leaving about $\frac{1}{4}$" of coat on the poodle; the No. 10 blade takes the hair down to about $\frac{1}{8}$" and can be used after the No. 5 blade if a shorter finish is required; the No. 15 blade is excellent for clipping of face, feet and tail of the usual pet poodle,

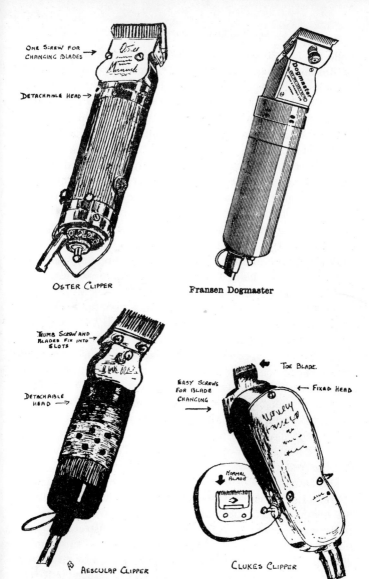

Diagram 29 – Types of electric clippers suitable for beauty parlour work.

while the No. 30 gives a *very* close cut for face, feet and tail etc. for show dogs, but needs expert knowledge to use safely.

The actual clipper with detachable head costs about £14 while the blades cost approximately £2 2s per set (£2 15s for No. 5). But as the machine is 115 voltage it is essential to have a transformer for most normal voltages in England. This transformer costs £1 15s.

The Aesculap Clipper is also extremely efficient and slightly cheaper than the Oster. This has a very quick method for blade changing, in fact not even a screw driver is needed and the attributes of both these makes are so close that we think it is a matter of individual taste. The 5 mm. blade will cut the short hair on body in a Dutch clip, using the clippers *against* the hair, and the coat on a short Lamp clip using the clippers *with* the hair, while the 7 mm. blade will leave the hair longer and deal efficiently with matting. The ½ mm. blade is good for face, feet and tail, and the ¼ mm. for a *very* fine exhibition clip. The price of this clipper is £17 17s complete with one head, and additional blades cost about £2 8s.

The Forfex is a good working clipper with easily changed blades, again cheaper than the other two mentioned, the machine costing £14 5s with blades about £2 15s. The Clukés Clipper is a fixed head machine recommended for general light work, and I think the special advantage in this clipper is the very tiny blade which can be obtained especially for toe work which we have found excellent. The clipper costs £6, and the special narrow blade for toe work is £1 extra.

The Horstman Clipper is perhaps the lightest and quietest of the lot. The blades screw on, and a thumb lever controls the depth of cut. These are £8 complete. With all electric clippers it is essential to follow the maker's instructions with regard to maintenance and upkeep, but none of them is difficult if normal care is exercised. They can all be purchased through the Diamond Edge Company, of Gloucester Road,

Brighton, and usually hire purchase terms are available if required.

It may be found that the occasional poodle simply will not take to an electric clipper under any circumstances, and therefore it is advisable to have a pair of hand clippers by you. After electric clippers, these are very slow and rather difficult to manipulate and one must bear in mind that a *fast* action must be used with your hand in working the blades, but the actual clipper must be moved *very slowly* against the skin of the poodle. If the clipper is pushed quickly it will only pull the dog's hair and hurt him, and if the clipper itself is manually worked slowly, then one only succeeeds in cutting the hair in ridges and chunks. The Diamond Edge pattern is about the best, the No. 1 having a 2″ bottom plate and barrel spring with sizes 1 to 0000. The normal size for face, feet and tail of a poodle is 00 or 000. The price of this clipper is 30/7d. The No. 2 is a medium size with 1½″ bottom plate and more

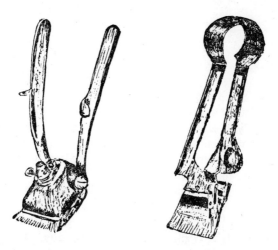

Diagram 30 – Two types of hand clippers.

suitable for fine work with blades 000 and 0000. Price 17/1d. No. 3 is designed for rough work, leaving the hair longer and is priced at 22/6d. (*see Diagram 30*).

HAIR DRYER: It seems that there is really only one suitable Hand Hair Dryer and that is the Forfex which we have found second to none. This costs £7 15s (plus £1 18 9d purchase Tax).

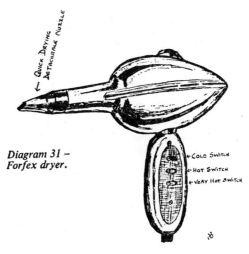

QUICK DRYING DETACHABLE NOZZLE

Diagram 31 –
Forfex dryer.

←COLD SWITCH
←HOT SWITCH
←VERY HOT SWITCH

It has three heats of warm, hot and very hot, and also a small metal gadget which fits on the nozzle and increases the blowing power if you wish to be extra speedy. Its only slight disadvantage is that it is a little noisy (*see Diagram 31*). The ordinary domestic hair dryer is not suitable for a Beauty Parlour as it is not made for sustained and regular work and when used for any length of time burns out. Another useful piece of equipment is a Fan Dryer. There are several of these on the market and they stand on the grooming table, giving a blow of warm air over the whole area of the dog. This has a dual use as it makes an excellent fan for very hot weather when

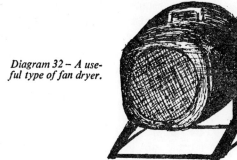

Diagram 32 – A useful type of fan dryer.

switched to cold (*see Diagram 32*). It is possible just occasionally to 'come by' an old-fashioned trunk dryer on a wheeled stand, of the type used many years ago in hairdressing salons. If you can find one of these they are very useful and when discovered can very often be bought for a song as they are now mostly redundant, and hairdressers are glad to get rid of them, having stored them in a cupboard for years. We were able to obtain one from a noted Court Hairdresser in Dover Street, London. This firm had long since ceased to use such antiquated methods, and its function when we discovered it was to blow up the boiler which was temperamental!

TOOTH SCALERS: A chromium plated scaler is an essential and these are available at about 15/- to 20/-.

NAIL FILES: Necessary for filing nails when show preparing a poodle. We recommend the very fine cross-cut file used by carpenters and available at a good tool shop. Cost about 2/- each.

HAIR SPRAY: A very useful rubber hair spray for fixing to the bath or sink taps can be obtained from either Boots or Woolworths at a very reasonable price, and is an essential for the efficient shampooing and rinsing of the poodle coat.

CONTROL FRAME: It is sometimes necessary in a Beauty Parlour to have some form of special control of the dog upon which you are working, and we would very strongly recommend a frame devised and manufactured by Mr and Mrs Glover of Stoke-on-Trent. As you will see from the photograph (*Plate 6*) this comprises a tubular frame, the legs of which screw firmly on to the grooming table. From the middle of the top bar hangs an adjustable chain to which is attached a leather sling which goes round the poodle's body, keeping him in a standing position. This is most useful in the case of the poodle who continuously sits or lies down or 'collapses'. On either side of the top bar is a hook on which a chain hangs, which clips on to the poodle's collar, thus preventing him from walking away. A few inches up the back of the frame is an adjustable wooden board which again prevents the dog from edging across the table away from you. The entire gadget packs away flat, is moderately light and most efficient, and is certainly the answer to the restless and fidgety dog. The support this gadget gives to the dog undoubtedly makes him more comfortable while being clipped or dried. It costs 47/6d and in view of the materials used and the time it would take to make, it would certainly pay one to buy direct from Mr and Mrs Glover. Their address is: 254 City Road, Fenton, Stoke-on-Trent. They also produce a very neat folding show table which is pictured and described in chapter X.

You will find a photograph (*Plate 13*) showing a great many of the items of equipment mentioned in this chapter which we hope will help you to recognise and pick the most reliable tools you will need.

Clients, when visiting the Beauty Parlour, may often ask for their poodles to be measured, and it is therefore useful to have by you a reliable measure. There are many designs in use, but not all are satisfactory. In Diagram 33 we have shown three types—the square measure set in even blocks and measuring 10″, 11″ or 15″ (as required) from the ground to the *underneath* of the top bar; the Hoop measure which is much the same type; and the Hound Measure which has a sliding top horizontal bar with the inches marked at the side on the vertical bar. In this latter measure there is a spirit level let into the top bar to ensure that the measure is not tilted when

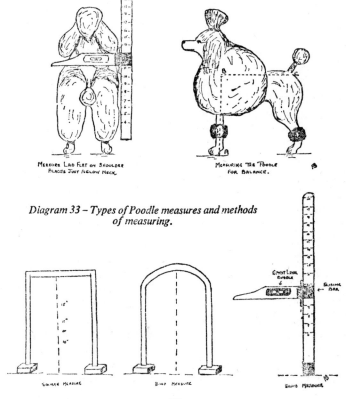

MEASURE LAID FLAT ON SHOULDER
BLADES JUST BELOW NECK.

MEASURING THE POODLE
FOR BALANCE.

*Diagram 33 – Types of Poodle measures and methods
of measuring.*

SQUARE MEASURE

HOOP MEASURE

SPIRIT LEVEL
BUBBLE

SLIDING
BAR

HOUND MEASURE

measuring. The first two measures are useful when you wish to ascertain that a dog is *under* a specified height and when using it one must be careful that both feet of the measure are firmly on the ground. The third type of measure ascertains the exact height of a dog in inches. The top bar of a measure should be placed flat on the top of the poodles' shoulder blades with the feet of the measures firmly on the ground or table, and in the case of the Hound measure the spirit bubble must remain dead centre when the top bar is on the poodle. Be sure that the poodle is standing squarely, with his front legs quite straight to the ground, and his hind legs in a relaxed and steady position. If the front legs are in any way extended out to the front or his hind quarters are even slightly crouching, this may make as much as $\frac{1}{2}$" to 1" difference in the recorded height. If you have poodles which are destined for the show ring, measuring should be part of the normal training routine, so that when the dog is measured by judges or stewards this is quite a natural procedure for him and he is quite relaxed. Thus the correct height is easily arrived at with no fuss. Poodles who are suddenly confronted with a measure are quite often apprehensive about it, and then either crouch or arch their backs, and it is impossible to know whether they go under the measure or not, and as a result a show award may be lost. It is interesting to note that the well balanced poodle should measure exactly the same in inches from the floor to the shoulder (A to B) as from the shoulder to the root of the tail (B to C) in Diagram 33. Thus if a poodle measures more from B to C than from A to B, he is possibly either long in back or short on leg. The first two measures can easily be made at home or purchased at any large Dog Show, but accuracy of height is essential; the Hound Measure can be purchased for approximately £2 and the one we use was manufactured by Mander & Co. of Margate, Kent. A good Saddler can usually obtain one for you.

In conclusion, it really *is* worth setting yourself up with equipment of a reliable nature which is manufactured by the people who have studied the problems attaching especially to the treatment of dogs. One can ' make do ' with gadgets designed for other uses, but if one can possibly afford it, it pays good dividends to buy the equipment which is produced particularly for heavy and constant wear which prevails in the busy Poodle Beauty Parlour.

Author's note. Since writing this book, Messrs. Fransen Ltd. have brought out an excellent new de luxe clipper in their ' Dogmaster ', which is a great improvement on the ' Forfex '. The clipper only weighs 25 ounces, and is extremely high powered being available in 200/250 volts or 100/130 volts, either A.C. or D.C. There is an extensive range of cutterheads running from coarse for winter coats to the finest cut for show work, and the existing cutterheads for Forfex will also fit the new Dogmaster. It is an expensive clipper but gives value for money. Price £23 5s for machine *without* cutterheads, and the various cutterheads range from £2 14s 6d to £3 6s 6d. There is also a small toe blade which is a great advantage.

CHAPTER TEN

Conclusion

Nails, Teeth, and Ears – Coat Conditioners
Overseas Conditioning Hints – Show Preparation – Show Hints

IN this concluding chapter, we want to talk a little about the remaining treatment which the really 'well-dressed' poodle must have. Such things as tipping, nail cutting and filing, cleaning of teeth, which all show dogs undergo as a matter of course, and which really do add the finishing touches to the poodle's beauty. We also include a few tips which have been useful to us in the past.

NAIL CLIPPING: This is not difficult though many dogs do not like having it done. There are one or two different types of nail clippers and without any doubt at all, we recommend the Guillotine type (which you will see in the diagram in the first chapter). Even the most fussy poodle doesn't object to a manicure with these. The usual type of nail clipper really does hurt the dog as the blades so often crush or bruise the nail, whereas with the Guillotine type, the actual cutting blade is thin and very sharp and it cuts the dogs' nails as though cutting butter. Of course it is easier to cut the colourless nail than it is to cut the black nail, because in the first you can see the pink quick in the nail itself. With black nails we suggest you take off a small piece and then file down to the proper length as there really is no way of knowing how far down the quick really is. You will see that you should press the actual pad and nail between the thumb and forefinger of your left hand and use the nail clippers sharply and decisively with your right hand (*see Diagram 34*). Pressing the nail and pad ensures a good steady grasp and also deadens the nerve in the nail for the

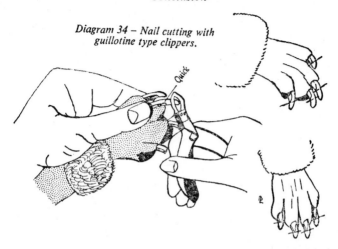

Diagram 34 – Nail cutting with guillotine type clippers.

moment. If by any chance you should cut too close to the quick and the nail bleeds, you can stop it instantly by dipping the nail straight into ground Permanganate of Potash crystals. When filing·the nail, the same pressing grasp should be used, and with your right hand file the nail *upwards.* At first you will find that you do not get the nail very short, but if you file the nails regularly once or twice a week the quick recedes (rather as in the case of someone who bites their nails) and the poodle will soon acquire a lovely foot, well muscled up with neat short nails.

TEETH CLEANING: Again a bit of a trial to poodles – or indeed any breed of dog – but a necessary procedure. Very efficient and easy to use dental scalers are sold, and we have had ours, which originally came from Spratts, for many years. They are now about 15/- each. If your poodle is inclined to get a certain amount of brown tartar on his teeth, this can easily be removed, *if you don't neglect it,* with a scaler. Look at Diagram 35 and you will see that the action of the scaler is

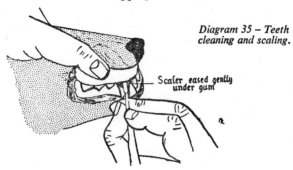

Diagram 35 – Teeth cleaning and scaling.

Scaler eased gently under gum

to gently push the sharp edge just under the edge of the gum and give a little pull or scoop. The sharp edge of the scaler then loosens the tartar and it will come off in quite big flakes. It is essential for a dog not to have tartared teeth because this state does lead to pyorrhoea and gum shrinkage, loss of teeth, and of course the breath of a dog with furred teeth is generally anything but sweet.

If your poodle likes large bones to chew this does more good to his teeth than anything. After scaling, the teeth should be well scrubbed with a solution of $\frac{1}{2}$ Peroxide of Hydrogen and $\frac{1}{2}$ ordinary cows' milk. This solution makes and keeps the teeth beautifully white. An occasional clean with damp cotton wool and a good tooth powder is also a good idea.

We would like to add a few tips for those of you who are exhibitors. Most of you may know them but perhaps some may find something new in them.

CARE OF EAR FRINGES: How often does one see a show dog who has good leathers, but the fringes are tattered? If you want your dog to have really sweeping ears, it is worth taking a little trouble, and wrapping them in thin polythene certainly grows the hair. Possibly the greatest advantage is that while wrapped up, the fringes will not dabble in the poodles' food and water, he will not drag them in the dirt while sniffing about, nor will he be able to chew them or lick them when they get food stained. It is quite a simple procedure and the dogs do not seem to mind wearing ' curlers ' in the least. Wrap each ear in a piece of thin polythene about 8″ × 6″, so that it wraps up to about eye level and extends about one to two inches below the fringe. Turn up the ends of the polythene including the fringes of the ear and place a small rubber band on the end of the roll (*see Diagram 36*). *But be very careful indeed that the rubber band is well clear of the actual leather*. If the band is put on the flesh part it will stop the circulation within minutes and you will cause the dog great pain and also damage the ear leather. Another good protection tip is to make small anklet covers in either calico or mackintosh which can be slipped over the anklets on the way to the Show when it is wet and muddy. It is best to

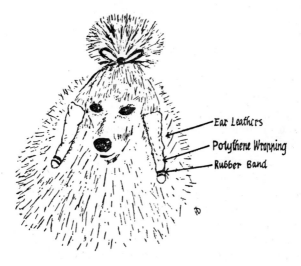

Diagram 36 – Protected ear fringes.

Diagram 37 – Showing use of a stocking cap for protecting ear fringes.

make these with hooks and eyes or tapes to fasten, although I have seen them with elastic top and bottom, but this again is terribly dangerous and can cripple a dog if it is too tight.

If you do not wish to wrap up your poodle's ears, another very good way is to take a thin nylon stocking, just the toe and heel and about three or four inches of the leg part. Cut off the end of the toe part, slip the stocking over the dog's head so that it fits round the head just above the eyes, enclosing the ears, the leg part circling his neck. This is an excellent arrangement for when he is feeding. Incidentally we always pop a stocking cap on our dogs when clipping feet and legs, as it prevents the poodle from dropping his ear fringes on to the parts you are clipping – a little habit they often have when objecting to foot clipping since they are intelligent enough to know that the trick makes it well nigh impossible for you to clip them! (*see Diagram 37*).

You have probably experienced the difficulty of putting a bow on your poodle's top-knot at a show, and have found your hand is shaking, the dog is all over the place, and anyway you cannot get the bow to ' sit ' straight. We always used to make our bows up at home, stitching them at the back so that they did not come untied, and then stitching a small gold safety pin on the back of the bow (*see Diagram 38*).

Conclusion

Diagram 38 –
Showing top-knot
bow.

Then when you finally do your poodle's top-knot for the class, slip an elastic band on the hair first and then pin the bow on in the front. It stays neat and tidy and never moves. For those wretched whiskers that will escape from the top-knot and form a fringe over the eyes, it is a good idea to take a damp sponge (just a tiny cosmetic one) with you, and smooth the hair back with this. It works wonders, and is better than any ' sticky stuff ' which is not allowed.

Another tip for the indoor show. You may find when you arrive that the floor is normally used for dancing and thus slippery. Dogs' feet skid and their action is affected. If you have a small block of resin (the type used for violin bows), rub a little of this on your poodle's pads and you will find he will be completely sure footed. Another good show gadget is the portable Show Grooming Table. This is made and retailed by Mr and Mrs Glover, who also make the Control Frame. It combines a light and steady folding table with a box drawer for all your grooming kit and show accessories, and is a most useful addition to your show equipment (*see Diagram 39*).

A last word about growing and conditioning a coat. Frequent bathing with good quality shampoos and Lanoline conditioners helps tremendously. This ensures that the poodle's coat is always in a clean condition with the pores free of dirt. Grease and dirt clog the pores of he skin and this creates poor growth and dullness. We have found that olive oil given internally does wonders for a slow-to-mature coat. Start with $\frac{1}{2}$ a teaspoonful over the food, increasing gradually to as much as

*Diagram 39 – Portable
show grooming table
with box drawer.*

a tablespoonful a day. Also as an external tonic, great benefit
is derived from the application of Cod Liver Oil. If the coat
is dry, brittle and lustreless, give an all over dressing with
this oil, and the method of application is to part the hair in
layers and paint each layer sparingly with Cod Liver Oil
with a very small stiff paint brush. Leave the oil on for three
days and then shampoo the dog. Repeat again in seven days
time, and so on until results begin to show. It is a messy
procedure but well worth the trouble.

The following is a coat treatment which is extensively used
in the United States on winning dogs, and was given to us
by Mrs Wohl, direct from Mr Larry Downey who is one of
America's top professional handlers. Mr Downey (who
handles the celebrated Mossoaks Poodles for Dr and Mrs
Zachary Wohl and has steered their lovely Champion Rothara
the Ragamuffin and Champion Rothara Merrymorn Nell
Rose amongst others to many Best In Show awards) manages
to combine wonderful presentation and top honours with
the greatest love for the poodles in his care, and is well known
for his selfless devotion to his charges, and no doubt this
plays a large part in his great success as a handler. Mr Downey

says he conditions a poodle for the ring by using Shapley 63 Oil which has the following hundred per cent active ingredients: Petroleum Hydrocarbons, Sulphur, Olive Oil, Essential Oils, Oil of Turpentine and Zinc Stearate. It was originally manufactured to combat Sarcoptic Mange and Psoroptic Mange, and does an excellent job in dissolving loose dandruff scales. Like any oil this naturally causes the outer skin to peel, and forces the new hair to the top. After the coat has grown to the desired length, he switches the poodles over to Shapley No. 1 Oil which has the same ingredients but is a lighter oil. This is put on with a thick brush and the coat is parted to use the oil. Oil is not used on ears or top-knots but some of the oil does of course penetrate the entire body. The dogs are bathed out about a month before the show with a Rug Shampoo, for the feeling is that a poodle coat is more wool than hair, and if the shampoo is good for a woolen rug it should be equally good for a poodle. The shampoo is not put directly on the poodle but is sudsed in the water, and then the dog is put into the water. Liquid Lux is used, and followed by a Richard Hudnut Cream Rinse. Certainly the poodles in the American ring have enormous coats of eight inches and more, and from the above it appears that no possible trouble is spared in getting the very best into a coat (*see Plate 8*).

Another excellent coat conditioner and tonic comes from an exhibitor friend, Mrs Shallcross of Trottingwheys Poodles of Colorado, U.S.A. and we feel sure she will not object to our passing on her advice. She tells us ' Bathe the poodle with a protein shampoo that contains Lanoline, and then brush in an oil solution on the wet coat, by dipping a brush into a little oil. The oil solution is made up of four parts Castor Oil, four parts Olive Oil, four parts Lanoline Oil, and one part Oil of Cloves. Then dry with the dryer in the normal way, and the heat of the dryer will melt the oil into the skin and coat. The oil should be applied at least once a week, twice if possible, and the dog should be bathed every two weeks. When bathing the coat, use a shampoo that will remove oil, otherwise the dog's coat will be too oily. It takes five months to grow an eight inch coat. To dress the hair in the ring, use Foo-Foo Coat Dressing (we imagine that a good tonic spray would be the equivalent in England). Brush well in and then brush out. This leaves no trace and it brightens and hardens the coat. Spray the coat with a good recognised hair spray to hold in place, otherwise your poodle will look a mess! This is what we do in America.'

TIPPING: This is a most important finishing procedure. So often a poodle may have a very profuse and very long coat, but somehow it just fails to look neat and smart. This is the moment to ' tip ' the coat. To do this, comb the mane towards the ground on each side in layers, starting with a layer from elbow towards hip. You will find the ends of the hair are a little straggly, so cut about $\frac{1}{4}''$ off the end. Then do the same with the next layer until you have worked up to the top of the back. Do the same on the other side. Then start on the chest working up in horizontal layers until you come to the short clipped part of the neck under chin. When all the slightly straggly ends have been tipped off, the coat should have a dense, close and beautifully rounded look. This procedure of tipping *must* be done when the coat has been shampooed and is standing up well, otherwise it is difficult to avoid ridges in the final result. Never tip any hair off the ears, they should remain with the hair on the fringes as long as possible.

Eyes need little attention, and a wipe over with cotton wool soaked in warm water keeps them clean and bright. For eyes that have a tendency to weep a little, a good tip is to bathe them daily with a solution made up of a teaspoonful of common salt dissolved in a cup of warm water. Or alternatively, Witch Hazel or else cold tea are excellent. But the poodle with running eyes is usually not quite as fit as he should be, and quite often the cause is a slightly acid condition of the stomach. For this a daily dose of Milk of Magnesia is often effective, or one of the herbal preparations containing Chlorophyll. Of course, the cause may equally be a blocked tear duct which is a case for the Vet.

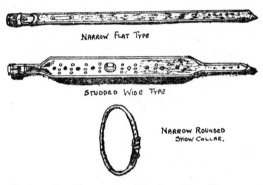

NARROW FLAT TYPE

STUDDED WIDE TYPE

NARROW ROUNDED SHOW COLLAR.

Diagram 40 – Three types of Poodle collars. The narrow flat type, the wide studded collar, and the narrow round collar.

While we are on the subject of special coat production, the matter of collars is most important. The poodle in the short clip such as Dutch Clip or Lamb Trim may wear one of the attractive wide poodle collars, but this type of collar is fatal for the poodle in either Lion Clip or Show Puppy Clip as it will quickly break off the long hair round the neck. If you intend to show your poodle or put him into Lion Clip, you should fit him up with a very thin rounded leather collar, as narrow as possible (*see Diagram 40*). But in any show clip, collars should only be worn when absolutely necessary, and should never be left on for long periods or overnight.

A small proportion of poodles suffer from car sickness which can be most upsetting for the dog and very upsetting to you if you arrive at the show with a dog who has dribbled down a beautifully prepared chest! Mrs Margot Roy of 93 Barn Hill, Wembley Park, who attends to the shipping of all our dogs for export and is second to none in this sphere, recommended some excellent little tablets called ' Cocculus ', prepared by Epps, Thatcher & Company of 60 Jermyn Street, London. Two of these tablets before setting out on a journey work wonders. They are homoeopathic, and are completely harmless. But if there is a danger of sickness or dribbling a small bib made of calico or towelling is a good tip. Make this so that it ties loosely round the neck, covers the chest, and is fastened with two more tapes round the body. It will ensure that the poodle arrives in a clean and fresh condition (*see Diagram 41*).

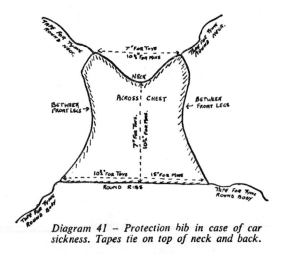

Diagram 41 – Protection bib in case of car sickness. Tapes tie on top of neck and back.

Starch is an excellent over night treatment before a show in the case of white poodles. Liberally shake the starch well into the coat, then let the dog shake and put him to bed. Next morning before the show, brush his coat very thoroughly so that all trace of the starch is removed. (It is against Kennel Club Show rules for a poodle to enter the ring with starch or powder in his coat.) You will find that the starch has toughened the texture of the coat and every hair is standing out well, and your poodle is looking brilliant. Starch is also an excellent dry cleaner if your poodle's anklets get grubby on the way to the show. This, of course, only applies to white poodles. There are excellent mist sprays prepared by ' Vitacoat ' which tone up the coat of the black, brown or silver poodle.

The poodle is a truly elegant creature and if properly cared for and artistically clipped, is a thing of tremendous beauty. But outward beauty is not all that is needed. To be really beautiful the poodle must also be happy. He must always be handled with gentleness and must never be frightened when being groomed or clipped, and this applies from the moment he is first gently combed at a month old. A frightened or apprehensive poodle can undo all the skill and artistry you have put into your clipping simply because he will then slink along and generally appear hang-dog. So be as gentle as possible and make him feel he really is in spirit the gay, friendly, fine looking chap that you have tried to make him look with skilful clipping. Poodles are very proud – and really very vain – and like most women adore to be told how nice they look in their new outfits!

Finally, we feel we cannot stress too strongly that only the best produces the best. If you want to get to the top in winning and presentation, *and stay there*, then you must be prepared to give your dogs the best. It is no good economising and skimping over food. If your dogs are to make a name for themselves, they must be given the food which contains most nourishment – plenty of good red meat, eggs, milk, and also comfortable housing conditions. No dog who is poorly fed, kennelled in dirty surroundings with no comfort, and whose nerves are on edge through any feeling of uncertainty – whether it be caused by those who look after him, or by the dogs with whom he has to live in close proximity – is going to give of his best when the big moment comes. So if you want the top, you have to give your dog everything that will make it possible for him to be the proud, happy, jaunty fellow who is such a joy to watch striding in for those First Prizes and Best in Show awards. And if you have done your part in his conditioning, both mental and physical, then you can feel it is a true partnership and you will really deserve both his and your success.

Index

Index